"Are you insane?" he growled.

"That was a very foolish thing you did," he continued. "You could have gotten us both killed."

Catherine stared at him in disbelief. "You're serious."

"Damn right I am. I had enough to worry about without your trying to play hero."

"Heroine," she corrected. "And I was trying to save your stupid life."

"Did you see me going down for the third time?"

"I never saw you come up the first time! And another thing . . ." Catherine stopped as he started to laugh. "What's so funny?"

"Us. We're having our first fight."

"No," she said grimly. "What we're having is our last good-bye."

Dear Reader,

Spellbinders! That's what we're striving for. The editors at Silhouette are determined to capture your imagination and win your heart with every single book we publish. Each month, six Special Editions are chosen with *you* in mind.

Our authors are our inspiration. Writers such as Nora Roberts, Tracy Sinclair, Kathleen Eagle, Carole Halston and Linda Howard—to name but a few—are masters at creating endearing characters and heartrending love stories. Their characters are everyday people—just like you and me—whose lives have been touched by love, whose dreams and desires suddenly come true!

So find a cozy, quiet place to read, and create your own special moment with a Silhouette Special Edition.

Sincerely,

The Editors
SILHOUETTE BOOKS

JUDITH DANIELS

The Sun Always Rises

Silhouette Special Edition

Published by Silhouette Books New York

America's Publisher of Contemporary Romance

In Loving Memory of Danny O'Brien

SILHOUETTE BOOKS
300 East 42nd St., New York, N.Y. 10017

ISBN: 0-373-09389-6

First Silhouette Books printing June 1987

America's Publisher of Contemporary Romance

Printed in the U.S.A.

JUDITH DANIELS

tries to incorporate her desire to write with her love of the performing arts. A seasoned movie buff, she believes that the motion pictures of the thirties and forties capture romance with a flair, a quality she tries to portray in her own novels. Although she has traveled throughout thc United States, Judith is settled in Tulsa, Oklahoma.

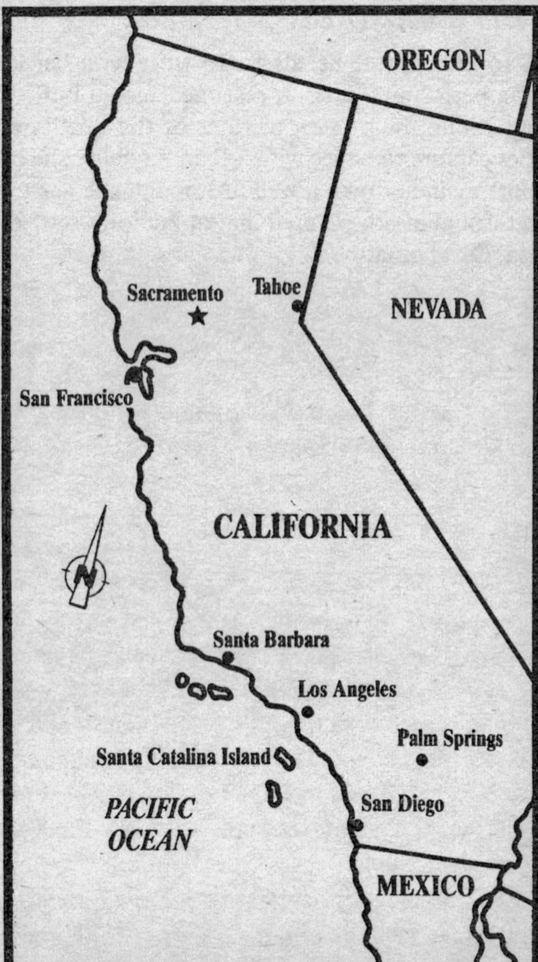

OREGON
NEVADA
Tahoe
Sacramento
San Francisco
CALIFORNIA
Santa Barbara
Los Angeles
Palm Springs
Santa Catalina Island
San Diego
PACIFIC OCEAN
MEXICO

Chapter One

Catherine Harrington searched the sky above the palisades. She was anxious for the dawn, but there was no hint that it would arrive ahead of schedule. Glancing at her watch, she realized the first light of day was only then sneaking through the city's back door in Angeles National Forest. She resigned herself to being patient. The sunrise had a long journey before it would spill into the Los Angeles basin and then wind down the canyons to reach the beach where she waited.

The fluorescent blue light of predawn was Catherine's favorite time for her morning walk. There was usually no one else on the beach, save an occasional early surfer, and so it allowed her time to think, to reflect, to assess. She usually savored every moment, but the approaching day felt different somehow, and it filled her with apprehension.

There were plenty of reasons to suspect impending danger. The salt air was unseasonably cool, and the waves were breaking too far from the shore. There was also a noticeable absence of gulls on the beach. But despite the physical evidence, Catherine could not convince herself that the real danger was the weather.

There was something more, something inside her. The winds of change were blowing through her mind, and it scared her slightly. Catherine had never been one to sit back and just accept what life had to offer, but lately she had done just that; she had become too comfortable with her life. It was time to move forward, toward the new day, toward the sunrise.

Suddenly the obtrusive sound of a car drew her gaze down the craggy walls of the palisades to the Pacific Coast Highway. A shiny but old Chrysler station wagon, loaded with surfing gear, slowed and then turned into the parking lot at the front of the pier.

"Crazy kid thinks he can surf in that," Catherine mumbled. Then, noting the distinctive woodwork along the sides of the vintage car, she added, "A Woodie! Must be a crazy rich kid."

Jealously guarding her solitude, Catherine decided to put more space between herself and the surfer. As she walked north toward the huge city pier, foam nibbled at her toes and carried in the frothy bubbles were bits of abalone shells that tickled her bare feet. The ebb line was reaching higher on the sloping sand and she had to move farther inland to keep the hem of her skirt from getting wet.

It started slowly. One large chunk of shell slammed into her legs. Then, a few seconds later, another, and then another and another. Catherine stopped and stared out at the vast expanse. There was an ominous darkness clinging to the horizon. A squall line was forming at sea, and the wind was creating swells that were growing larger with each set of waves. Until that moment, Catherine had only heard of storms that churned the ocean violently enough to pull up debris from its floor.

"Morning," a deep voice called.

Catherine jumped and turned toward the sound. Expecting to see a typical California golden boy, she was pleasantly surprised by the man walking toward her. He was the surfer, but he was certainly not typical, nor was he a boy. Instead of the awkward muscles of youth, his tall physique had the guarded restraint of someone who had been an athlete for many years.

The solid muscles of his wide shoulders allowed him to carry an eleven-foot board and an array of other equipment as though it were all a tiny satchel. His sinewy arms glistened with golden hair on skin that was an even darker shade of gold, and where the black wet suit veed low on his chest there was another patch of topaz-colored hair.

"Good morning," she finally managed to answer.

He stopped a few yards away and laid his brightly colored board on the tawny sand. "Do you think I can get a halfway decent ride out of those waves?"

Catherine turned to study the water, which she already knew was too hazardous for anyone less than a professional. The breakers had not changed, they were still sculpting the shore like an angry artist in a fit of rage.

"As a matter of fact," she said, turning back to face him, "I think it would be too dangerous." Her last word was spoken in a soft gasp of shock as she discovered he had quietly moved and stood alarmingly close to her.

At such a short range he was physically overwhelming, and also vaguely familiar, but then wasn't everyone in the Hollywood area vaguely familiar? It seemed that everyone had been, was currently or was hoping soon to be an actor, and since her business catered to the entertainment industry she decided she had probably seen him at the restaurant.

He had the type of looks that could not be easily forgotten. She especially liked the tiny scar that formed a half-moon on his right cheekbone. It was only as long as a thumbnail, then it disappeared into his beard. He had a mustache and a full beard that curled around his jawline, and a head of thick blond hair to match. Although the beard added a special ruggedness that was compelling, Catherine felt cheated. She wished she could see all of his face. More than that, she wished she could see his eyes, but he was wearing reflective sunglasses.

That was when she saw it, the sunrise mirrored in his silvery lenses. "Oh, look," she said, turning toward the cliffs. "The sun is coming up."

He stood beside her, and they watched the light show in silent awe. It was beautiful, but even the spectacular colors could not dim Catherine's awareness of the stranger. His nearness caused a faint stirring inside her, and she felt compelled to sneak another look at him. As she turned her head to bring him into the line of her vision, her stolen glance was caught. He was already staring at her.

She should have been embarrassed. She should have looked away, but she didn't. Instead, Catherine stared back at the stranger. His face was the type a movie camera would love: strong yet sensitive, rugged but edged with just enough vulnerability to be captivating. She wished more than ever that she could see his eyes and wondered if the reflective glasses were purposely worn to allow no access to the man behind them.

He smiled, ending the moment before it became too awkward. With a nod of apology, he stepped back. "I didn't mean to bother you," he said, turning abruptly and walking back to his board. He bent down, picked up a triangular piece of fiberglass, then faced her again. "I'll just attach this fin to the bottom of my board and get out of your way."

It could have ended there. In fact, Catherine told herself, it should have ended there. She should have smiled and walked away. Instead, she stayed. He intrigued her.

From her vantage point several feet away, Catherine tried to peek over his shoulder. "Is that a sailboard?"

He glanced up, giving an easy smile that infected her with a lazy warmth. "Yes ma'am. Are you a boardsailor?"

She shook her head and hesitantly moved forward. "No, but I've always wanted to learn. I had a friend who said it was like skiing on a mountain that moves with you. He was going to teach me, but—" Her voice caught in her throat. Quietly she finished, "That was one of the things we never got around to doing."

Friend! She had called him friend. Why? True, he had been her best friend, but more than that, he had been her husband. Why was it still so hard to say she was a widow? Catherine felt bittersweet as myriad memories began to play through her mind. She stared straight ahead with glazed eyes, seeing only the past. For a moment a vision of her husband with his dark curly hair stood before her, then the image was replaced with a blond giant. When she blinked back to reality, the stranger's hand was lifting her chin so he could look into her eyes.

He frowned. "Are you all right? You turned so pale."

Catherine drew in a shaky breath. "I'm fine," she answered, but the look on his face said that he didn't believe her. "Really," she added, trying to sound convincing.

In a gesture that surprised her, he removed his sunglasses and studied her. His eyes were brown, as brown as the dark earth of Topanga Canyon, and the look he gave her was just as untamed as the countryside surrounding the canyon road. But there was also a tenderness in his regard that made Catherine feel warm inside. Feelings that had lain fallow for too long were aroused, and Catherine knew it was time to distract her own thoughts.

She pointed to the rigging he had been working on. "With the condition of the water, wouldn't a semifloater work better than a slalom board?"

His eyes widened. "I thought you said you'd never been windsurfing?"

"I haven't, but living at the beach, I've picked up a little knowledge of the sport," she said. "I'm right, aren't I?"

"Oh, yes," he said, taking her arm to lead her back to his gear. "You're quite right." In spite of herself, she flinched at his touch. If he noticed her behavior, he didn't let on. "Actually, a semifloater, or even an asymmetrical would perform better out there today."

They stopped and Catherine bent down to look at the paraphernalia he had deposited in the sand. "You should have brought all your sailboards."

He clasped his hands together behind his back and rocked to and fro. "Maybe I can't afford more than one board. They're very expensive, you know."

She looked up at him and squinted into the morning sun. "I saw your car. Money is no problem for you."

"A very astute observation."

"Not really. Woodies have been pretty sought after ever since Jan and Dean sang about them. A wagon in as good a shape as yours is a real collector's item."

"Oh," he said, as though he had never realized that fact before. "Why?"

Catherine knew he knew, but she played along. "Because they only made a thousand of them before World War II closed down the production lines."

"Nine hundred and ninety-six to be exact."

Catherine shrugged. "I was never very good with numbers."

Admiration shimmered in his brown eyes as he spoke. "It appears I misjudged a lot of things I've found here this morning."

He extended his hand to help her up, but he did not release her after she stood. It was a simple thing, her small slender hand in his large callused one, but Catherine's reaction to him was anything but simple. His touch was like an electric charge that pulsed through her veins, and her body felt radiantly alive again.

What had begun as polite friendliness had grown into a dangerous game. Catherine knew she needed to break the spell he so easily cast on her, but she couldn't think clearly enough to know how. Finally, the man took the initiative and released her as he bent and began to gather his things.

Still slightly stunned, Catherine watched him for a few seconds before realizing what he was doing, then she spoke in a voice of disbelief. "You're not going out there with the wrong board, are you?"

He was already heading for the water, and he stopped to flash her a smile. "I want to try a different combination. I think I can get more maneuverability out of this."

Catherine shook her head. "I think you'll maneuver yourself right into a hospital bed."

He winked. "I love a challenge."

She watched him walk waist deep into the surf before she called after him. "Be careful!"

"Careful isn't fun."

For an instant she was carried back in time. Her husband used to say the same thing. Thoughts of the past fought again for their right to invade her, but Catherine was determined not to give in this time.

When she snapped out of her daze, she saw the brightly colored sail had been hauled up the mast. A gust of wind snapped the slack from the sheeting and the surfer began to sail.

The predatory manner in which he roamed the whole length of the wave made him appear hungry for it. He had spoken the truth: he thrived on a challenge. Quickly he utilized the largest wave in the set, catching it just ahead of the curl. Catherine watched him carve an S down the face of an advancing wave, then when he reached the base of the swell, he reversed directions.

Working back toward the power, he climbed to the steepest, most critical part of the wave. With the mastery of a world-class sailor, he shredded off the top making a bank shot by jibbing his board at the crest. The lip sent him flying out over the water.

In midair, with a mighty twist of the board, he lifted it from underneath himself and grabbed the rig in a quick manner that pointed his sail downward. He worked the sail and succeeded in prolonging his hang time as Catherine held her breath. Her heart nearly stopped, as she watched the jump pull him across thirty feet of water.

His strong aggressive style was beautiful to see. Equally as beautiful was the analytical approach he took, leaving very little to chance. He followed the natural contours of the water, yet at the same time he tried to force his own will onto the wave. He could not possibly make it bend to his demands, but still he tried, and Catherine realized he was a man who was used to getting his way.

Nick O'Donovan circled around and positioned himself where he could study the fury that was building in the distance. The sky toward the horizon was rapidly growing darker, and sheets of gray rained from the clouds into the sea. The storm was moving parallel to the shore. It would have to change directions to move inland, but Nick would stake his reputation as an outdoorsman that it wasn't going to do that.

He looked into the opaque haze on his right side and then to the bright sunlight on his left. He was straddling an imaginary line that Mother Nature had drawn between her two worlds that morning. Although he couldn't explain why, he felt as though he were trespassing in a place that was not meant for mankind. There had been many times in his life when he had found himself alone with the incredible force of nature, and like now, it always left him overwhelmed.

This was the source. Since the beginning of time, this was what artists, composers and writers had tried to assimilate. In his opinion, they had failed. The power and beauty he saw around him was something that had to be felt more than seen, and that was why it could never be truly captured.

Nick looked across the tumbling expanse of water to the shoreline. The auburn-haired woman was still watching him. He drew his eyebrows together as he remembered his fierce attraction to her. She was lovely, but even that could not explain his immediate fascination with her. He had grown up in Hollywood, surrounded by the world's most beautiful women, but there was something unique about this one.

Watching her at dawn made him wonder what she would look like in other kinds of light. He imagined on a cold winter day she would be warm and comforting, but in the heat of summer she would look cool and inviting. The shadows of dusk would remind him that she was his and his alone. And the night? Even candlelight could not dim the passion he would see in her green eyes.

Nick shook his head as if to clear it. When he met women at the beach so early, they were usually perpetually tanned nymphets, rather shallow, and easily impressed. They would talk awhile without really saying anything. After a few coy giggles he would play out the scenario and ask for a phone number.

Then he would file it away with a meaningless promise to call her someday.

What a ridiculous ritual, he thought. But she wouldn't play that type of game. She was different, and that difference was what drew him to her. It also made her very dangerous.

A woman like that would smother him, and that was a real shame. He let his gaze wander back toward her. She was slow poison all right, but the package she came in tempted him to give it a try.

Bending low he hoped the cold spray would slap some sense into his thoughts. Suddenly he was caught by a strong gust of wind, and Nick realized he was on the edge of a new set of waves that promised to be tremendous. Damn! He had been so busy thinking about her that he had allowed this to sneak up on him without being ready. He was only a split second off, but it was just enough to make the ride end hazardously.

The set had more power on its face and more water breaking on its lip, a classic surf capable of lacerating a fallen sailor. Nick knew that one misjudged jibe and the wall behind him would tear the boom from his hands, but still he continued his trek to the top.

He was amazed at his own deftness as he started the setup for his jump. It would be beautiful or tragic, he couldn't predict which since he had never gained control of the wave. Then he felt it start to break and knew he had made an error. With a curse he realized he needed to pull out. But it was too late. He couldn't get through. He had mistimed the jump, and the lip was going to pulverize anything in its path.

An avalanche crashed down on him in an explosion of angry white water. The mast was snapped in two as though it were a tiny twig, but when part of it hit Nick's forehead, it felt like a redwood tree. Dazed, he struggled against the onslaught that followed.

The ripped sail was now only shreds of color. Nick and the board were sucked down into a swirling abyss, then they were shoved violently upward. The board was shot like a missile toward the beach, but Nick was sent flying backward in a full spread eagle.

He hit the water with an excruciating thud that sucked the air from his lungs. Then a terrifying blackness surrounded him and stole his thoughts. When his mind focused again, he was curled forward in pain and looking at a liquid blue world.

He felt trapped in a dream where he couldn't wake up. His thoughts split as though his mind were displaced from his body. He was both the viewer and the participant. Part of his mind told him he had to reach the surface and the other part of his mind told him not to panic because it wasn't really happening. Instinct drove him toward the lighter blue water that had to be up; yet no matter how he struggled, he seemed only able to move in slow motion.

Seconds passed like hours, until he finally broke free of the watery prison. The Nick that watched from somewhere faraway cautioned him with logic not to gasp for breath. The other Nick ignored him; he was fighting for his life and he immediately drew in the much-needed air. A white-hot trail of fire burned down his windpipe and exploded in his chest. He screamed but there was no sound.

A voice, cool and soothing touched him. "Don't try to move yet."

He tried to look around, but his eyes were too watery from the salt and the pain inside him.

Again the voice came. "Just breathe, very shallow."

Nick squeezed his eyes into tiny slits, and then he saw her, rising from the sea like a mermaid in an ancient mariner's vision. No, she wasn't a mermaid; they were blond and wore no clothes. This creature had thick red hair, which hung in long damp curls around her face, and her eyes were like polished gemstones of jade. And she was clothed, though the wet blouse clung to her breasts like a second skin. He commanded his dazed mind to think whether he knew her. He should know her; he wanted to know her.

Her hands were like ice when she brushed back his hair and touched the bump on his forehead. The scorching ache in his chest had blocked all other pain from his mind until then. Now he could almost feel the lump growing larger with each beat of his pulse, and he understood why the pounding in his head would not cease. For the life of him, he could not remember how he had been injured. The only thing he did know was that he needed to get back to solid ground, quickly, before the last of his strength was played out.

"I have to try and move," he said, hoarsely.

Watching her green eyes as she surveyed the situation was the catalyst that fit the missing pieces into his puzzled thoughts. It all came back to him with horrifying clarity. He frowned. How could someone her size have fought the riptide to reach him? Suddenly fear gripped him. *My God, she'll never make it back on her own.* He had on a wet suit that retained his body heat, her arms and legs were exposed, and what clothing she did have on was probably more of a hindrance in weight than a help against the elements. Somehow he had to get her back to safety.

They were being tossed and pitched by the angry water, and he could see it was taking a tremendous effort for her to stay near him. Then a large wave caught them unaware and slapped them both beneath the surface. They bobbed back up, spitting water. Nick reached out, hoping he could hold her above the fury of the whitecaps, but his chest muscles responded with a sharp contraction. He moaned and collapsed on his side, curled in a tight ball.

She slipped her left arm around his neck and cupped her fingers beneath his chin. "Lean against me," she ordered, trying to support most of his weight on her left hip. "I have to get you out of here."

"Are you crazy?" Nick choked out his gravelly words in a wavering pitch. "You'll never be able to get yourself back to shore, much less me."

Catherine shot Nick a look that left no room for argument. "Don't fight me."

Grudgingly he nodded and relaxed against her. Immediately he became more buoyant in the water, and for the first time Catherine began to feel that she just might get him back to solid ground. Then he tensed again. She looked at him, ready to plead for his cooperation, but the terror she saw in his eyes stopped her words.

Before she could think, he had literally picked her up and shoved her forward. She glanced back and blanched upon seeing the huge mountain of water looming above them. Catherine reacted at the same time that he shouted his one word command.

"Swim!"

And swim she did, with all her might, but the rushing water picked her up almost before she started. For the breadth of a moment she thought they were riding high enough on the wave to slip over it—then it began to break. Tons of water spilled down on top of them. Catherine rolled with the turbulent energy as it threw her down toward the ocean floor. Her arms were flailing, and once she hit something so solid she knew it must have been the surfer, but she couldn't see anything except wild white water.

As quickly and as violently as the surf had poured down, it hit bottom and sprayed back up. The column of water rose like a phoenix taking Catherine with it. Then the breaker tossed her aside as though she were a toy it had grown tired of. She splashed down in a swell that was rushing toward the shore. Still being pitched around, she realized sand was scraping her bare arms and legs. She had made it.

Choking and coughing, she let the tide carry her the rest of the way in. Unceremoniously, she was deposited in a sitting position very near where she had entered the water. Catherine knew she could not stand and doubted she could even crawl. Her nerves were jumping as though she were still caught in the vortex of the adventure. Closing her eyes, she tried to calm herself.

Leaning on her elbows, she found she was too weak to support herself and fell on her back. As she lay within the tide line a thin film of icy water remained beneath her. With her wet clothes and the biting wind, Catherine began to realize she was freezing. She knew she should move, but every inch of her body ached with the effort it took to just lay still and breathe.

With an alarming jerk, she remembered the surfer and sat up. He was struggling to walk out of waist-deep water, but the onslaught of waves kept pounding him to his knees. The second he stumbled, Catherine was on her feet rushing to him. With his arm over her shoulder and her arm around his waist, they tried to walk, but when he leaned against her, the weight was too much. Weakened by what they had just been through, they toppled down on the sand after three steps.

Catherine ended up on her back. He landed on his stomach, on top of her. His face was buried in the wet ringlets above her shoulder and his breath came in white-hot gasps against the side of her neck. Their legs were intertwined and his hard muscular chest was burning a lasting impression against her breasts. She had to move.

Feeling her stiffen, and anticipating why, he mumbled an order into her ear. "Lie still."

More than anything, she wanted to just lie back and relax for hours, maybe days, but something inside her would not allow that luxury. Her arms were pinned to her sides, forcing her to push up with her chest as she wriggled her hips in an effort to free herself. It was useless, she couldn't move him. Worse than that, the gauzy material of her skirt and blouse provided no protection against the sensations her fruitless efforts had created.

He grinned weakly. "Okay, don't lie still."

"Would you kindly get off of me so I may get up?" Catherine asked, trying to put a little dignity into a situation that had none.

"No."

"And why not?"

"I'm too exhausted to move."

Catherine rolled her eyes. "And whose fault is that?"

"Yours."

"Mine! Are you insane?"

He groaned as he placed his hands on the sand and lifted his upper body so he could stare down into her eyes. "Look, lady, that was a very foolish thing you did."

"A foolish thing I did?"

"Yes, you could have gotten us both killed."

Catherine stared at him for a moment in disbelief. "You're serious."

"Damn right I am. I had enough to worry about without you trying to play hero."

"Heroine," she corrected. "And I was trying to save your stupid life."

"Did you see me going down for the third time?"

"I never saw you come up the first time. And another thing—" Catherine stopped as he started to laugh. "What's so funny?"

"Us. We're having our first fight."

"No, what we're having is our last goodbye," she snapped, then realized her line should be followed by a dramatic exit.

Nick smiled. "Is this where you're supposed to get up and walk away with dozens of violins accompanying you, and I'm supposed to chase after you as we cut to a commercial?"

She laughed. "Yeah," she said, "something like that."

He shook his head. "I don't have the energy."

"Neither do I."

"Good, because I have a better idea." He leaned closer, and the soft whiskers of his blond beard tickled her cheek. "Let's kiss and make up."

She could have turned away, but there was a gentle hope in his dark eyes that made it all seem right. His mouth met hers with a tentative touch as though he expected a static charge. There was only warmth.

Catherine felt the smile on his lips as he deepened the kiss. She smiled, too, at the delicious tickle of his beard and mustache. He tasted of the sea, and she felt drawn to him, like the ocean to the shore.

The moment, the man, and the feelings were magic. She wanted to let go of her lifeline on reality and drown in the enchantment he wove so delicately, but then her mind took charge. Magic was only an illusion, and happiness only something that preceded sadness. She opened her eyes and pulled away.

A quicksilver memory flashed before her. The agony of the past year crashed hard upon her. She knew it was totally unfair, but in that moment, Catherine hated the man beside her. He had made her feel again and had thereby dredged up all of her shipwrecked dreams.

With new resolve, she realized she had to free herself of this man before more memories jumped out of her past, before it was too late to hide the tears that were forming. Her enormous burst of strength caught him off guard and Catherine knocked him off her. Then she was on her feet and running.

"Hey, wait!" he called after her.

Catherine had no intention of waiting. He'd come dangerously close to awakening emotions she'd thought were dead, and she ran because she intended them to stay that way.

Chapter Two

It was late afternoon when Nick wheeled his Woodie onto Sunset Boulevard. "Let's see," he muttered to himself, "I can take the Glendale Freeway to the Hollywood Freeway, then pick up the Pasadena Freeway by Dodger Stadium and take the Harbor Freeway... no, no, not the Harbor... no... yes, it is the Harbor that loops over to the Santa Monica Freeway."

The blue Chevrolet in front of him sped up in an attempt to beat the yellow light and make it across the five lane intersection. Nick glanced at his watch, growled at the time he'd wasted and decided to sneak through the light on the Chevy's tail. As Nick sped up, the Chevrolet's driver suddenly changed his mind and slammed on his brakes. Nick and the driver behind him who was following his lead had to violently stomp on their brakes.

At the wrenching squeal of tires, Nick braced himself to be sandwiched between the two cars, but the sound of crunching metal never came. When he realized he was not going to die, he threw up his arms. "O'Donovan, you're a fool to come back to this rat race. You are not cut out to be an urban dweller." He shook his head. "I should have stayed gone another two years."

Picking up a napkin, he glanced at the list of chores for the day he had scrawled. The ink of the felt-tip pen had bled to the point that even he could no longer read most of the words. Nevertheless he knew every task, and none of them had gone the way he had planned them over coffee that morning.

Opening up his house in the Hollywood hills had been filled with bothersome details that he despised. He could handle anything that came up when he was in the wild or sailing the seven seas, but his mind was not geared to handle household details like hiring a maid or having the electricity turned on or off. He had been reminded of his lack of domesticity when he'd opened the refrigerator and found an amazing assortment of moldy shapes that had once been food.

After the unexpected, but necessary purchase of a new refrigerator, Nick had gone to the next stop on his list, his business manager, Sidney L. Dinsmore III. Sidney's office was in the Bradbury Building in downtown L.A., and like the historic landmark, which was filled with imported marble and lacy French grillwork, Nick thought that Sidney was too polished and showy. Sidney had one thing in his favor, though, he was the best business manager in town, and Nick was smart enough to know that when it came to his money, personalities didn't matter.

Fortunately their personalities didn't have a chance to clash that day, because Sidney had been out of his office. So Nick had moved on to his next stop, the marina. He knew if he didn't sell his boat, it would always be a temptation for him to sail away whenever the city started to close in on him again. The consignor said they would have to take less than Nick's asking price, and Nick had agreed, realizing she wasn't worth quite as much if he subtracted the sentimental value.

The *Dangerous Lady* had been a good sloop. Together they had seen the most fascinating ports of call, and out on the ocean, all alone, they had talked. She was the best kind of lady to have. She never gave a differing opinion, she just listened and nodded with the breeze. In fact, it had been the *Dangerous Lady* who had agreed with him when he'd asked himself if it wasn't time to return home and to try to settle down to a normal way of life.

Suddenly, without warning, as had happened so many times that day, the woman on the beach came to mind. "Talk about a dangerous lady," Nick muttered as he conjured up a mental image of the way her wet clothes had clung to the sensuous curves of her body.

He smiled, remembering their encounter. Just one more thing on his list that hadn't gone right. He had driven to the beach hoping to surprise his best friend, Gideon, but when he had found no one home, Nick had decided to take advantage of the surf. He had never expected to take advantage of a beautiful woman.

The minute she'd turned around, he had experienced an odd sensation. Nick knew there was no such thing as love at first sight except in the movies. And even if such a ridiculous thing did exist, it could never happen to Nick O'Donovan. He labeled his feelings as merely fascination at first sight. She was special—potentially hazardous—but special, and like a fool, he'd let her slip away without knowing her name.

Suddenly horns blared behind him. Nick glanced up. Seeing the green light he waved and stepped on the gas. Again his mind returned to choosing the best route. "There's another way. I used to take it and it's a little faster...if I could just remember." He brought the heel of his hand up and smacked his forehead. "Think, O'Donovan, think. You haven't been gone that long."

Glancing up he saw the familiar white and green highway sign. "That's it! The Golden State Freeway, then I only have to switch off twice." He started to turn and head up the entrance, but pulled up short when he noticed that traffic was backed all the way up the ramp, and nothing on the freeway was moving. "Oh, hell. I'll take Sunset all the way to the shore."

Nick laughed at his own play on words. That's where he was going, Gideon's restaurant called Sunset at the Shore. A restaurant! The thought still amazed Nick. It had seemed so unnatural for Gideon to buy a restaurant; he had always been such an outdoor person, like Nick.

Until a little more than two years ago, the two men had done everything together. In high school they had both excelled in track and field. There had even been talk of either or both of them as Olympic hopefuls, but the escalation in the war had overshadowed that dream.

In the jungles of Vietnam it had been hard to dream of anything except freedom. Freedom to make their own choices, to go where they wanted when they wanted. They had vowed that whatever happened, they would remain together and find that personal freedom. And they did.

When they returned to the States, they sort of stumbled into their careers, but before long Nick and Gideon were known as Hollywood's most daring stunt team. Their expertise had afforded them the best jobs, or gags, as they were called in the industry, and the best money. Better than that, their careers had allowed them to travel between jobs. It was the perfect setup, or so Nick had thought, until suddenly, two and a half years ago, Gideon had decided to retire.

Nick slapped the wheel of his Woodie. "Stuntmen don't retire," he said, repeating the same thing he'd said at Gideon's unexpected announcement. "We slow down a bit, we take less dangerous roles, but we never, never retire. And we never do something as sedentary and mundane as buying a damn restaurant."

Nick gave an evil-sounding laugh as he imagined how tired and disillusioned Gideon must be after all this time of frying hamburgers and slapping mustard on foot-long hot dogs. Yes, Nick thought, Gideon will be more than ready to reunite the team of Harrington and O'Donovan, especially when he heard Nick's plan for a new action sequence. Excitement coursed through him and he shook with anxious anticipation. Soon it would be just like old times for the two of them. No, it was going to be even better.

A few minutes later Nick pulled into the lot in front of Sunset at the Shore. He knew his plan was in trouble when he saw a uniformed parking attendant waiting at the entrance. The freckled-face boy made no attempt to hide his surprise when Nick stepped out of the Woodie.

Following the boy's gaze, Nick looked down at his outfit. He wore a khaki bush vest over a royal-navy Yukon shirt and his favorite pair of walking shorts. The shorts were original Number 10 Ducks, which were no longer available, and therefore the British tan shorts were quite ragged—even the patches needed patching. The hiking boots that he sported could grip anything, and to attest to that fact a clump of earth was still attached to one sole. Rubbing his chin, Nick was pleased that he'd had the foresight to neatly trim his beard that morning, but then he remembered what he had forgotten to put on his list: a haircut.

With a laugh, Nick asked, "Do you think I'm overdressed?"

The teenager lifted a thoughtful eyebrow. "That would depend, sir."

"On what?"

"If you're famous or not?"

Again Nick laughed. "Far from it."

"Then you'll never get away with it. Henri is very strict."

"Henri?"

"The maitre d'."

Nick frowned. "Gideon said he was going to remodel the place, but I never expected he'd go this far."

The boy squinted into the sun, which was just starting its descent into the ocean. He cleared his throat, sounding a bit hesitant. "I take it, you haven't been here in awhile, sir?"

"No, and it's been too long, apparently. The last time I was here, the place catered to the beach crowd, and a coney was their finest delicacy." He looked at the converted warehouse, which was lit like a Hollywood premier. "Nothing stays the same, does it?"

"No, sir," the attendant said, starting to give Nick's keys back to him.

Nick held up his hand to stop the boy. "Park it," he said, grabbing his desert hat by the brim and taking it off. He ran his fingers through his unruly sun-bleached hair, then pulled the hat back on with determination. "I'm going in."

The boy gave him a questioning look. "You're either the bravest guy I've ever met or the dumbest."

"I'd like to think I'm the bravest," Nick said, then winked. "The truth is, I know the owner."

The boy's cockiness returned as he tossed the keys in the air and caught them. "But, you have to get past Henri to get to the owner."

Nick started toward the door. "No problem."

A look of disbelief crossed the boy's face. "I won't park her very far away, sir."

Cheeky kid, Nick thought, and made a mental note to give him a generous tip. Something about the boy reminded Nick of himself when he had landed his first job as parking attendant at one of the snazzy restaurants on La Cienega Boulevard.

Nick opened the tufted lavender door and froze, half in and half out. When the door swung shut, it nudged him into the foyer as he stared beyond the entrance hall. He felt as though he had entered a time warp and had been transported back to an MGM sound stage. The best sets of Busby Berkeley, Vincente Minnelli and George Sidney were combined into one giant room of glamorous Technicolor.

"Pardon, Monsieur," said a haughty voice, "but we do not give tours."

Nick stopped his survey of the dining area and glanced at the small man who had suddenly appeared in front of him. He laughed at himself. "I guess I do look somewhat amazed. I just didn't know Gideon was creative in anything except at staging stunts. This is damn close to being impressive."

"You are correct. Monsieur Harrington did lack imagination. The decor was done by Madame Catherine."

"Oh," Nick said, suddenly catching sight of several movie stills that lined the hall. His mind drifted as he smiled at a grouping of spectacular stunts that he and Gideon had performed in a variety of major motion pictures.

Henri's voice was condescending. "If it is dinner you seek, may I suggest Barney's Burger Barn next to the all-night fishing boats. It's just down the beach at the city pier. You see, we do require proper dress, monsieur, and this—" he let his gaze sweep over Nick's attire "—this is not proper."

"That's okay," Nick said, still looking at the pictures. "I'm not here to eat."

"Then may I inquire as to why you are here?"

"Huh? Oh, yeah." He finally glanced back at the maitre d'. "I'm here to see Gideon."

A small gasp escaped Henri. "I'm afraid that is quite impossible."

As Nick opened his mouth to argue, the telephone on the desk began ringing. Henri excused himself and motioned Nick to be seated on the sofa by the door. Acting as though he had lost the battle, Nick paced around the vestibule, but as Henri became involved with the call, Nick hurried into the dining room.

He ignored the curious looks of the patrons, thinking only of the look he would see on Gideon's face. A smile of triumph spread across Nick's face as he opened the door to the office. The smile faded immediately when he saw his business manager. "Sidney?" Nick questioned in surprise. "What are you doing here?"

Sidney automatically jumped to his feet and assumed a stance worthy of a B-Western shoot-out. The thought of Sidney L. Dinsmore III in the Old West was absurd and Nick laughed as he spoke. "Relax. I checked my gun at the door."

Sidney's hands were trembling as he straightened his gray flannel vest and tried to appear unshaken. "Good grief, Nick, you scared me half to death. Don't you ever knock?"

"Sorry."

Sidney froze suddenly as the reality finally hit him. "Nick? Good Lord! It is you. You're back."

Nick flicked the brim of his hat with his forefinger and nodded with a grin.

Suddenly Henri was behind Nick. "A thousand pardons, monsieur. He slipped by while I was detained." A bony hand grabbed Nick's collar. "I will escort the intruder from the premises at once."

Nick stifled his immediate reaction to deck the man and turned his glare on Sidney. "Call off this French poodle, or I'll flatten him like a crepe."

Sidney sighed. "Let him go. I'll handle it from here."

Reluctantly Henri released Nick and looked around the office. Henri nodded toward the open door to the apartment behind the restaurant. "But what about Madame Catherine?"

Sidney went to the door that led to Gideon's apartment and partially closed it. Turning back toward Nick he had the look of a man who was about to pronounce someone's death sentence. "I will take care of it, Henri. Please, leave us alone."

The maitre d' quietly exited back into the restaurant and closed the door behind him. Nick shoved his hands into his pockets and stared back at the man across the room from him. They were the same age, but that was where the similarity stopped. Sidney was the epitome of the west coast Yuppie, a fact only made tolerable by his business prowess.

"I'm not very good at small talk, Sidney, but I think the usual dialogue would be for you to say something like: welcome back, O'Donovan. You're looking well, the sea air must agree with you. Then I'll say something like: you're looking good, too, Sidney. The gray at your temples is a nice touch, it's almost distinguished."

Sidney folded his arms across his chest. "Forgive me if I'm not as enthusiastic as you'd like, Nick."

"I'm not looking for enthusiasm. You didn't approve of my sailing around the world when I left, and obviously you still don't. All I can say is, I felt it was the right thing to do at the time, and in retrospect, I still feel that way."

Sidney leaned on the mahogany desk between them. "Mind if I ask you something, O'Donovan?"

Nick moved around behind the desk and looked at Gideon's new chair. He sat, testing the comfort, then laced his fingers together at the back of his neck and leaned back, propping his feet on the desk. "Ask me anything, Sidney."

"Why didn't you respond to my telegrams?"

Nick was rummaging through the magazines on the bookcase behind the desk. "Geez, what's the deal? All I can find is *House Beautiful* and *Redbook*." He glanced up at Sidney. "What telegrams?"

The color drained from Sidney's face. "Surely you got them."

"Nope. Hey, where's Gideon's *Sports Illustrated*?"

Taking an initialed handkerchief from his pocket and dabbing at his forehead, Sidney slowly walked to the other side of the desk and sank into a chair. He began muttering, more to himself than to Nick. "Two. We sent two."

"Two what?" Nick asked, still searching for something readable. "Oh, two telegrams."

Sidney seemed barely able to talk above a whisper. "Yes. We sent one to Bora Bora and another to Tahiti, in case you had already left the first port."

Nick stopped and faced his business manager. Sidney always was a bit melodramatic, but this was no acting. Sidney was genuinely upset. "Bora Bora," Nick repeated. "That was over six months ago."

"Ten to be exact. Didn't you get either of them?"

"No. I didn't follow the itinerary I'd left with Gideon. I sailed to New Zealand from Bora Bora." At the troubled look on Sidney's face, Nick shrugged. "That was the whole point of the cruise, to be free to follow the wind and the tide and my own thoughts."

Sidney sighed. "I can't handle this. I'm no good at it."

"Can't handle what?" Nick said, growing more interested and irritated by the minute.

Sidney glanced toward the apartment door and mumbled, "But it wouldn't be fair to Catherine, if I didn't try to...."

"Who's Catherine? Gideon had just met a girl named Catherine right before I left, is it the same one?"

"Yes." Sidney drew his gaze from the ceiling. "Oh, Nick. There's so much I need to tell you."

"Then tell me for pity's sake! Nothing can be as bad as you're letting on."

Sidney shook his head. "It is, and I don't know where to begin."

"Spit it out," Nick said, his voice growing louder. "Start anywhere. No, wait. I'll start for you. What happened, did Gideon finally get hitched?"

"That's a rather crude way of putting it, but yes. He and Catherine were married a little over a year ago."

Nick placed the back of his hand against his forehead. "Oh, excuse me while I faint. Such horrible, such shocking news." Suddenly he realized Sidney wasn't smiling. Finally believing in the seriousness of what Sidney was trying to say, he asked, "There's more, isn't there?"

Sidney nodded. "Please, sit down, Nick. What I have to tell you is . . . most unpleasant."

From her apartment behind the restaurant, Catherine heard the commotion in her office. She didn't stop to put down the papers she had been gathering for Sidney as she hurried toward the partially closed door.

"Sidney," she called, "is something wrong?" Rounding the doorway, she looked up. Her next sentence died in her throat.

"You!" she gasped in unison with Nick.

She looked into his dark eyes and, flustered, Catherine dropped everything she was carrying.

Nick bent down at the same time as she did, and he winked at her. She looked away quickly, and busied herself by gathering the documents. Catherine apologized for her clumsiness, but she could not hear her own words over the pounding of her heart.

He began picking up the papers, too, but he never took his eyes off her. Deliberately tilting her head, she let her hair fall forward to hide her face from his stare. When they reached for the same piece of paper, their hands touched. The contact was brief, but it forced their eyes to meet again. She saw a mixture of confusion and happiness in Nick's eyes and knew the same emotions had to be reflected in her own.

Taking her elbow, he helped her stand. His gaze held her spellbound, until slowly, another thought worked its way into her mind: Sidney was staring at them.

"I don't think you two know each other," Sidney said. "Catherine, may I present Nick O'Donovan. Nick, this is Catherine Harrington."

Panic crossed their faces at the same moment. Then there was a long moment of silence. Catherine's gaze wandered to the wall behind her desk, where she had another set of pictures of Harrington and O'Donovan. She had spent so many stolen moments staring at them, but it had always been Gideon that she saw, not the man beside him. All she really remembered from the pictures was that Nick was tall and blond. Even now it was hard to realize it was the same man; he hadn't had the beard before.

Releasing his hold on her arm, Nick stepped away. "I—I had no idea."

"Neither did I."

"You had no idea of what?" Sidney asked, confused.

Neither of them answered Sidney as Catherine extended her hand in an obligatory gesture. Her voice was soft, and unexpectedly husky. "Welcome home, Nick."

He shook her hand. "Damn. Gideon always has all the luck."

Catherine swallowed back the sadness. Gideon's luck had run out by the time she'd met him, and she felt a momentary jealousy that Nick had known him when he was riding the crest of life and had everything to look forward to.

"About this morning . . . " Nick started.

She gave a nervous laugh and shook her head. "From the stories Gideon told me, you acted within character."

"Good Lord," Sidney interjected. "He's not the beach bum you told me about. Is he?"

Nick waved Sidney off, keeping his eyes on Catherine. "I hope you can forgive me. I'm really sorry, not for kissing you, only for letting Gideon find you first."

She smiled. "Gideon said you were a charmer."

"He kissed you?" Sidney asked, his voice unusually high. "You didn't tell me that part." Then he turned to Nick. "You kissed her?"

"Speaking of Gideon," Nick said, ignoring Sidney, "where is the old rascal? I need to apologize for—" he paused and looked at Catherine with regret "—for admiring his wife so blatantly."

She looked at him in horror, then at Sidney. The look on Sidney's face confirmed her worst beliefs. Nick didn't know. *Sweet Mother of God, he didn't know.*

A tortured emptiness swept through her, and she grabbed her stomach, feeling sick. She had to tell him, immediately. It wasn't fair to let him go on believing one more minute, but she wasn't sure that she had the strength. "Nick," Catherine said, motioning toward the sliding glass door, "would you step out on the deck for a moment?"

Sidney rose from his chair, but Catherine held up her hand to stop him. "This is something Nick and I need to discuss, alone."

The relief was obvious on Sidney's face as he eased back into his chair. "I'll be here if you need me," he offered as Catherine followed Nick outside.

The restaurant was housed on pilings that extended beyond the beach into the ocean. It was the only building on the small private dock, but there was hardly more than a walkway of timber leading to the office and apartment at the rear of the pier.

Nick was leaning against the railing and staring out at the amber sun which was setting in a golden sea. "You know, when Gideon bought this place, I was envious. Oh, not of the restaurant, I thought that was a dumb idea and I told him so, but I was extremely envious of the location. It's absolutely beautiful here. I told him it was like living on the edge of forever."

Catherine knew that Nick was only talking to delay the inevitable. She needed to tell him, but there was no easy way to say it. Words were so useless. Nothing could soften the blow; nothing could change the suffering. The one man who loved Gideon as a brother and should have been the first to know, was the last.

"Gideon's dead," she said.

It came, just as she had expected it would: that look. She had seen it so many times, but it had never been so intense.

He tried to laugh. "I must have heard you wrong, I thought you said that Gideon was—" He stopped, unable to complete the sentence.

"You heard right, Nick."

She saw panic fill his eyes and knew his thoughts were darting in a thousand directions. He was denying it. He was telling himself that if he did not dwell on any single thought too long, then reasoning could not take over. But it would; it always did.

He began to pace back and forth on the deck. Suddenly he stopped and looked at her. "It's a joke. It's all some sort of practical joke and Gideon is hiding somewhere around here laughing at me." He started circling around. "Come out, Gid. Enough is enough. You've had your fun," he cried, swinging his fist at an unseen target.

Catherine caught his wrists and held him still for a moment. When he made eye contact, she spoke. "It's not some horrible joke, Nick. No one could be that cruel."

The bitter accusing stare came next. "You're lying," he said, throwing his hands up, easily breaking Catherine's hold on him. Then he grabbed her shoulders and gave her a shake. "Tell me you're lying."

She didn't answer. She didn't have to. She knew what was coming. Slowly, with finality, he accepted her words for what they were—the truth.

Catherine had braced herself for anything to happen next, but his silence was unexpected and it broke her heart. He was so lost, so unprepared to grieve for another human being.

He released her as devastation took over his body and left him weak. He looked toward the edge of the day and shook his head. "He should have sailed away with me. I should have made him come."

"It wouldn't have made any difference, Nick."

With the suddenness of a summer storm, anger flashed across his face. "No!" he cried, "No!"

Catherine touched his arm, but in his anguish Nick didn't temper his strength as he flung her away. She stumbled backward and would have fallen if Sidney had not stepped from the sliding glass door and caught her.

Nick turned and ran the length of the pier to the parking lot, then he vaulted to the beach below. Catherine tried to rush after him, but Sidney would not release her.

"Let him be," Sidney said, quietly.

Catherine watched Nick run away, and she shed the tears that he could not.

Chapter Three

The hours passed slowly, until finally the restaurant began to close, and still Nick had not come back. Catherine sat next to Sidney at the bar, but her thoughts were wandering around L.A., trying to imagine where Nick would have gone.

"Mrs. Harrington," a voice called from the entryway.

Catherine turned and faced the parking attendant. "I thought you had already left, Thad."

"No, ma'am. I was just about to finish the lockup and I was wondering," he paused and held up Nick's keys, "what should I do about these?"

Sidney was on his feet heading toward the boy before she had to speak. "I'll take the keys," Sidney said, escorting Thad to the door.

Catherine listened to Thad's "good-night." Then there was the familiar sound of the bolt on the front door, followed by two footsteps to the light panel, then silently, swiftly, the dining-room lights dimmed to a single beam above the bar. A memory stirred inside her, unknowingly. Sidney had followed the same routine as Gideon always had. How strange that remembering something so simple, so ordinary, should fill her with so complete a joy.

"What are you grinning at?" Sidney asked, coming back into the room.

In the dim light, she saw herself reflected on the mirrored wall; she was smiling. "This was our favorite time of the day. Gideon and I used to sit here and talk for hours."

Sidney glanced around, then rolled his eyes. "If you ask me, with the lights low, this place is just plain spooky."

Catherine could feel herself drifting into the past, even her voice sounded faraway. "Gideon liked the way the shadows huddled around the edges of the room. He said the shadows were like lingering ghosts of the people who had been here."

"Lingering ghosts? Yuck!" Sidney recovered from a shiver and took his seat at the bar again. "Speaking of people who have been here and gone, are you ready to give up hope on O'Donovan?"

"Nick," she muttered, drawn back into the present. "Did you call his house?"

"Yes, Catherine. I told you, his phone hasn't been reconnected yet."

"Did you call—"

"I called everyone. I called the Stuntman's Association, and they weren't aware he was back in town, he's still listed as inactive. I called Spencer Lord Productions, but no one there has heard from him. I even called Spencer a little while ago at home and woke him up. No one, I repeat no one has heard from Nick."

She frowned, then brightened as a thought came to her. "The marina. Maybe he took his boat out."

"I called there first. I figured he took off once, he could do it again. They told me he put the *Dangerous Lady* up for sale today, and they hadn't seen him since. They promised to call if he showed up." He placed his hand over hers. "Catherine, he's not going to come back here."

She snatched her hand back and looked up defiantly. "I think he will."

Sidney's eyes widened. "How can you be so sure about what he will or won't do? You only met him this morning."

"But I've known him for a very long time—through Gideon."

"Then you should know that Nick can take care of himself. He's been doing it for thirty-six years."

"So I've heard. But tonight is different. Wherever Nick is, right now, he's hurting deeply. I know what he's going through, I've been there."

"We've all been there," Sidney said.

"Not quite. Oh, I know that you and Spencer and all of Gideon's friends miss him, but not in the same way I do."

"Of course not."

"And not the way Nick will. Gideon and Nick were like brothers, closer even because theirs was not a bonding by blood, but by choice. They placed their lives in each others hands, time and again. That makes for a very special relationship."

Sidney waved her off. "Aw, all the stuntmen say that. It's some sort of brotherhood they develop with each other."

"Nevertheless, Nick has just lost his best friend and he needs someone to talk to, but the only person he feels close enough to is Gideon. And he can't talk to Gideon because losing Gideon is the whole reason for his pain."

Sidney swirled the clear liquid in his glass then downed the last of his gin and tonic. As he placed the glass back in the same water ring on the counter, his voice was flat. "So what are you proposing?"

"Nothing. I'm not proposing anything. I'm merely stating a fact."

"Okay, I grant you that Nick is grieving right now, but why do you want him to come here to you?"

"It's obvious," Catherine said, spreading her hands in the air. "He needs a friend, Sidney."

"But why you? Why must you be the one who comes to his rescue? Do you think you can just ride in and take Gideon's place as Nick's best friend?"

"No one can take Gideon's place, but I can become a new friend."

"Even if he does come to you, which I doubt he will, it won't work."

"Why not?" she challenged.

"You know why."

"No, I don't."

"Catherine, men and women can't be friends like a man and another man, or like two women."

"That's ridiculous," she said, turning to stand.

"I agree," Sidney said, pivoting his stool to follow her movements around the room. "Nevertheless, Catherine, it's true."

She stopped to absently brush at a nonexistent crumb on a table. "Oh, Sidney, I know I'll never have the kind of friendship the two of them had. Still, I feel I should try."

"Well, you're right about one thing," he said, his voice forecasting his sarcasm. "You won't have the type of relationship they had because Nick didn't try to pick Gideon up the first time he met him. And I'll wager my entire portfolio that they never kissed."

Angrily, she stuffed her hands into the pockets of her skirt and turned away, but then another thought skittered across her mind. "Sidney," she said, turning back to face him, "you're jealous. Aren't you?"

"Me? Jealous of Jeremiah Johnson incarnate? Don't be ridiculous."

"Well, I hope you're not because it would be totally unfounded. Becoming Nick's friend doesn't mean I'll stop being friends with you."

"I know that," he snapped. "I just feel that this is the wrong time for you to get involved with someone."

She smiled knowingly. "I'm not going to get involved with him. I only want to be his friend."

"Let me be his friend. You stay clear."

Catherine blinked in surprise. "You? I didn't think you even liked him."

"Of course I do. I don't understand him, but I like him."

"That's the difference, Sidney. I think I do understand him. Besides, I promised Gideon."

"Nick has a reputation. He's a wanderer. You'll get burned, Catherine."

"Rubbish."

"I know what I'm talking about, Catherine, you're too vulnerable right now."

"I know you mean well, but . . ."

Suddenly Sidney bolted straight up. "Shhh!" he said, bringing his finger to his lips.

"What?" Catherine asked in a loud whisper.

"Did you hear that?"

"I didn't hear anything. What did it sound like?"

"I'm not sure."

Catherine had circled back to the bar, and she shrugged as she rested her elbows on the counter. "It was probably nothing. Strange noises are a way of life on this old pier. It settles and creaks and things are always smashing into the pilings below."

"I suppose you're right," he said, but his posture remained rigid and his gaze darted nervously around the room.

"All the same," she said, patting his hand, "why don't we move into the apartment? It's more comfortable there."

"Oh, sure!" Sidney said, lifting his hands, palms up. "Let's go someplace where we'll really feel safe." He rose to follow Catherine into her office. "And that's another thing I wanted to talk to you about. Your apartment."

She shook her head and laughed as they moved through the office. "Sidney, my own mother doesn't lecture me this much."

"If she were here and saw your life right now, she'd be doing the same thing I am."

"That's precisely why she's not here," Catherine answered. "Anyway, I've never understood your objection to me living behind the restaurant. I'm actually better protected from the outside world than you are in your house in Coldwater Canyon."

Sidney opened the door to her living quarters. "I don't care what you say, it's not safe for a woman to live out here alone."

Catherine preceded him into the apartment. "Oh, Sidney, you're such a scaredy-cat." She flipped on the lights, then froze. Out of the corner of her eye, she thought she saw something move near the staircase. Making a quick study of the room, Catherine saw that nothing was out of place. Still, she could not shake the feeling that someone had been there.

"Is something wrong?" Sidney asked, coming up beside her.

"No. Just you and your horror stories. You have me jumping at my own shadow." She rubbed her arms. "Sit down and I'll fix you some of my famous herb tea. I guarantee it will relax you."

As she busied herself in the kitchen area, she glanced back at Sidney, who moved aimlessly around the apartment. It was one large room with nothing to define the kitchen, or dining and living areas. There was a sense of free-flowing space that extended into her loft bedroom. What Catherine loved most about the apartment were the three walls of floor-to-ceiling glass. Her view was as magnificent as the Pacific itself.

Sidney stared out at the black night and the ocean, which was even blacker. Catherine kept an eye on him as she placed her Chinese tea service on a bamboo tray. "Sidney, I appreciate that you volunteered to keep me company, but it really wasn't necessary."

He turned quickly to face her. "I'll always be here if you need me."

"That's sweet of you, Sidney. You're very kind."

"I know."

Catherine tried not to let her amusement show as she carried the tray into the living area. "But I wish you had gone to the Dodgers game like you'd originally planned."

"And I wish you hadn't refused to go with me. You're a stubborn woman."

"True." She poured the tea. "Are you still hearing noises?"

He faced her quickly. "Why? Are you?"

"No. I just noticed that you're walking around in circles. Something must be bothering you."

He loosened his tie. "It's this place. I don't know how you can stand to live here."

"Are we back to that?" She handed Sidney his cup. "I remember when Gideon added this apartment to the back of the restaurant. You said he was crazy."

"I didn't say he was crazy, I said he was mentally imbalanced."

Catherine sipped at the steaming amber liquid. "What could possibly bother you about a place as beautiful as this one?"

"I feel trapped here."

"With all this openness? Don't be silly."

"I'm totally serious." He dipped an almond cake in his tea and continued pacing. "Have you ever realized how cut off you are from the rest of the world?"

"Yes, and I like it that way."

"You're behind that huge building." He pointed toward the restaurant. "And at the very end of the pier. There are only two ways out of here: through the restaurant, or down that tiny walkway along the side of the building."

"Actually, there's a third way. You can dive into the Pacific."

He frowned. "And that's another thing. Everywhere you look there's water."

Catherine put her cup down as she finally surmised the reason for his protest. "Sidney L. Dinsmore III, you can't swim. Can you?"

"Nonsense."

"It's true isn't it? I remember now, at all our beach parties, you would never get in the water."

"Okay, okay. So I can't swim, big deal. But that's not why I don't like you living here. My fears are founded on facts."

Catherine stood. "Your facts can be carved in stone for all I care." She walked to the back window, folded her arms and stared out. In the distance was a wall of fog that would soon cloak the whole beach, but for the moment the brightly lit room was reflected on the surface of the dark water.

She felt an instant calm as she watched the waves gently rocking toward shore. The mirrored image of the room swayed like a movie effect that indicated someone was dreaming. "I love it here," she said, softly. "I feel free when I look out and see the ocean. It's like a constant friend. The only thing I can trust to always be there, forever."

For a moment the room was quiet, but it wasn't silent; it was never silent. As always, there was the crash of surf.

Sidney set his empty cup down and rubbed his hands together briskly. "And that again brings us to our less than constant friend, Nick. I think it's obvious that he's not coming back."

Catherine hated the defeat in her voice. "I suppose you're right."

"We've been sitting around here for hours. It's time you faced the truth." He stopped. "I'm right?" Then, with a tug on his vest and a quick nod, he added, "Of course I'm right. I'm always right."

Catherine moved away from the window. "Come on," she said, slipping her arm through his. "Which way do you want to go to your car, through the restaurant, down the walk, or by way of the ocean?"

"Very funny," he said, removing her arm from his. "Go ahead, laugh it up, but this is a very real problem."

"I'm sorry. I didn't mean to make fun of you, Sidney. You have a point, I guess. Even so, what can I do about it?"

"Move."

"Are you out of your mind?"

"No. I think you should move inland, or at least, on land."

"I can't." She extended her hand and made a sweeping circle of the room. "This is my home, Sidney. I could never leave here. Never."

"Is it the apartment you can't leave, or is it something else?"

She stiffened. "I don't know what you're talking about."

"I think you do."

He was right. Catherine knew exactly what he was talking about, but she couldn't admit it aloud. She doubted anyone could understand that the world was taking something very precious away from her. There was no way to stop it, but there, in her apartment—her sanctuary—she could at least try to slow down the inevitable. She was losing Gideon, a little at a time.

For a good while after he died, Catherine could talk about Gideon, and in her mind she could see him, all of him. His smile, his eyes, the way he'd stand when he was delivering the punch line of a joke. Then little by little, the picture had started to fade. She couldn't remember the exact shade of blue of his eyes. She couldn't see his smile, or remember what his laughter sounded like. The world was moving forward, and as it did, it was becoming harder and harder to hold onto Gideon. He was fading into a ghost of the past.

"Forgive me," Sidney said, as tears welled in Catherine's eyes, "I shouldn't have said anything."

"There's nothing to forgive," she said, refusing to give in to the tears.

"I just hate the thought of you wasting away out here."

Catherine tried to sound amused. "I assure you, I'm not wasting away. Now, you'd better get home and get some sleep."

He nodded and started toward the door, then stopped. "Oh, those papers I came here for. I still need them."

Catherine couldn't correlate her thoughts for a moment. "Papers? Oh, the papers, I forgot all about them." She pinched the bridge of her nose. "Was that just this afternoon? It seems like ages ago." She started toward her office. "It'll take a few minutes to put them back in order."

"Never mind, I can get them tomorrow, or have Bunny drop by and pick them up."

Catherine shook her head. "Doesn't your poor secretary have a name besides Bunny?"

"Bonita Lucita Montoya O'Brien."

She frowned. "Bunny it is."

Sidney leaned forward, kissed Catherine's forehead, then turned and started out the door.

"Sidney?"

He stopped.

"I may not always agree with you, but I do appreciate the fact that you care."

He nodded and left. Catherine slid the door closed behind him and stood for a second looking out at the wispy fog that was starting to drift into shore. She waited until his footsteps faded toward the front of the pier, then turned off all the lights, inside and out.

Facing the apartment again, Catherine saw that the room had become one with the blue-black world of water and sky. She smiled. "This is why I can't leave here, Sidney. Where else could I find such a beautiful place?"

She walked toward the stairs, but paused at the sofa table and stared at her wedding picture. "And where else could I keep the world from taking you away from me?"

Gathering the picture to her breast, she hugged it for a moment. Then, slowly, she continued toward the stairs. Yawning, Catherine began to realize she was very tired. It had been a long day since she had run into Nick on the beach.

As she took the steps one by one, she began to feel the effects of her exertion. Her body ached in unexpected places, and she accepted it as revenge for trying to play hero. Hero indeed! She laughed, remembering how Nick had bawled her out for trying to save him. Her next thought hit her with a jarring thud: the man on the beach had a name.

Suddenly, everything was different. No longer could she think of the surfer as someone she would never see again. He was her husband's best friend, and she had been attracted to him. She'd kissed him! Even after she had run away from him, she had found herself drawn to the window in the hope of seeing him again. Now he had a name. It was Nick, Nick O'Donovan. Gideon's best friend. The ramifications staggered her as she reached the top of the stairs.

Slowly, she crossed the loft to her dressing table and dropped onto the stool. She pulled the picture away from her breast and looked at it. An empty ache swept through her. She knew the two smiling people in the photograph were herself and Gideon, but it didn't feel like them. It was as though she was looking at two actors she'd seen in a sad old movie.

She stared and stared and stared. And she told herself, if wishing could make it happen, when she looked up she would be able to visualize Gideon again. But glancing into the mirror, all she saw was the disappointment on her face. Beyond tears, Catherine propped her elbow on the vanity and rested her chin in her hand. That was when she saw it. The patio door was open. She froze. The dark form standing beside the door was a man.

Chapter Four

For a split second Catherine couldn't believe she was actually seeing someone and she tried to blink him away. When she opened her eyes, not only was he still there, but he was smiling. The eerie smile hung in the darkness, like a Cheshire cat's.

Suddenly, he moved. She screamed as one thought raced through her mind: the phone. The wedding picture crashed to the floor, and she knocked over the stool as she jumped up. She lunged for the bedside table and had the receiver in her hand when he grabbed her wrist.

"Catherine, it's me. Nick."

She wrestled his grip another second before his words soaked into her fear-stricken mind. "Nick?" she asked, looking up at him.

It was him, the man she'd longed to see since early morning. The same rugged features, the intriguing half-moon scar, but in the shadowy light all she could see of his eyes were two dark sensual pools. The pools glistened when he spoke. "Sorry I scared you."

"Oh God, Nick, it is you." She went weak with relief. The receiver slid from her hand and did a tap dance on the wooden floor as her legs buckled, and she sat on the side of the bed. Nick sat beside her and she leaned against his shoulder. "I'm so glad it's you. I was so worried when you ran off like you did."

"I should have called."

"Yes, and—" she stopped, suddenly realizing her heart was still racing from the fright he'd given her. Grabbing a pillow by the corner, she swung it in front of her and smashed it into Nick with a force that amazed even her. "You sorry son-of-a—"

"Hey, wait a minute," he said, falling back on the bed, shocked, but amused. "What happened to 'Oh, Nick, I'm so glad to see you'?"

"What do you mean sneaking in here and scaring me to death?"

Nick held up his hands in surrender, but Catherine's anger hadn't been appeased yet. She rose to her knees and continued assaulting him with the pillow. "You inconsiderate irresponsible jerk. How could you do such a heartless stupid thing?"

"Hey, I'm sorry," he said, dodging another blow. "Enough is enough."

Catherine was ready to back down when he made a fatal mistake. Laughing, he placed his forefingers together making a cross to ward her off.

"So you think this is funny, huh?"

"I said, I was sorry," he managed between laughs. "What more do you want? Blood?"

"Yes!" she answered, going after him with renewed vigor.

"Okay," he said, his eyes flashing. "You want a fight, I'll show you a fight."

He grabbed the pillow, stopping it in midair. Catherine's eyes narrowed, and she tried to jerk the pillow back. Nick lay, effortlessly holding it with one hand. Then, with a cocky tilt of his head, he gave one quick tug and Catherine landed on top of him with the pillow between them.

They were inches apart, and Catherine saw Nick's shadowed face as he pronounced each word slowly, "Let go of it."

"You let go," she countered just as adamantly.

"I'm giving you fair warning. Turn it loose or else."

"Or else what?"

"This!" he said, running his fingers up and down her sides.

Catherine burst into laughter. Her immediate reaction was to release the pillow from her grasp, but she recovered it before Nick could snatch it away. He attacked her ribs again, sending her into fits of giggles, but she refused to give in.

"Stop!" she choked out. "Stop it—I can't breathe."

"Then let go, Catherine."

"Never!"

His large hands played up and down her sides with an alarming quickness. She held her death grip on the pillow even when her whole body was limp from the tingling shivers Nick's hands were creating. But he was relentless and finally, she could do nothing but give in to complete uncontrolled laughter.

Nick pulled the pillow from between them and flung it across the room with a triumphant victory yell. Catherine was too consumed with laughter to notice when he had rolled her onto her back, but suddenly through her happy tears, she was looking up into his face.

In the darkness, she could see the glint of his smile and the dark rumpled outline of his hair. Nick was breathing hard and Catherine realized she was, too, but they were at odd rhythms, causing her breasts to strain against the muscled wall of his chest. The laughter died between them.

Catherine became aware of long forgotten feelings that were awake again. They were feelings she didn't want to admit, but feelings she could no longer deny. They snuggled deeper into the soft bedding as Nick pressed his body more firmly to hers. Slowly his lips came down to brand her with his white-hot kiss and flames of desire coursed through her veins.

On the beach, he had been tentative, testing, but tonight he wanted more, and she willingly met his demands. A shudder echoed through her as one delicious sensation after another was released by his deep penetrating kiss. She arched against him as they drew from each other's need.

It was just a kiss, a voice cried from within her, how could he take her to such heights with just a kiss? It was both wondrous and frightening. Catherine's arms went around his broad shoulders and she clung to him.

Nick pulled back. His body stiffened, but his eyes were a soft smoky brown from the passion still smoldering inside him. Then a cold veil swept over his warm gaze, and Catherine was confused by the angry look he gave her. With a muttered curse he rolled away from her.

He needed air. In a flash, Nick was outside on the balcony, but he still couldn't breathe because the night was heavy with fog. Feeling smothered, he lashed out. The gray curtain parted without a sound, then closed again, swallowing his hand as though it had been taken into another dimension.

Glancing up to where the moon had shone earlier, Nick saw no hint of light. He looked toward the ocean. The only clue that the sea still existed was a dull swishing sound that seemed to come from no particular direction.

Though he hadn't heard her move, Nick was suddenly aware that Catherine was near. Her perfume permeated the dense vapors and the fragrance teased his nostrils with a haunting memory. A dozen apologies and explanations filled his mind. None were spoken.

"Are you all right?" Catherine asked from somewhere beside him.

"Me? Yeah, sure. And you?"

"Fine."

The stillness was broken only by their breathing. Nick wondered which was heavier, the fog or the silence that hung between them. He swore to himself and slammed his fist into the palm of his hand. With any other woman, he would know what to do, or to say. Hell, with any other woman, he would not have stopped.

Turning toward her, Nick hoped to see at least a faint outline; there was only gray. "Catherine, I—"

"Don't say it, Nick. Let's just pretend the whole thing didn't happen."

He clenched his fists, then slowly, regretfully, he opened his fingers again. His voice was flat and too calm. "I shouldn't have taken advantage of the situation like that. I just—" he swallowed "—I just forgot who I was and who you were and who..." His head dropped to his hands and he whispered, "I just forgot."

"We both forgot," she said, "and that's what scares me."

Nick reached out into the fog, but he let his hand hover a few inches from where he knew she was. More than anything he wanted to touch her. He wanted to feel her and know that she was real. Slowly he drew his hand back. It was best that she remain just a voice in the darkness.

"Oh, Nick, in all this time I've never, for one single moment, forgotten about Gideon until... until we..."

He didn't want to hear what she was about to say. "Look, we're both adults," he said, stuffing his fists into the pockets of his jeans. "There's no need to blow this thing out of proportion."

She didn't respond.

"It was just a kiss. Right?"

There was a long silence.

"We were just two lonely people who lost someone they cared for very much, and we were just trying to make some sense of it all. You know, put a little warmth into this cold world."

"Is that what we were?" Catherine asked in a doubtful voice.

"Oh, hell, I don't know. I think I heard that in a movie once. See, I'm not very good at handling this type of situation." He tried to laugh. "In the movies, this is where the director yells 'cut,' and the star comes in for the close-up and the dialogue. I just do the spectacular stunts and somebody else does all the talking. I like it better that way."

A foghorn blared from the distance. Catherine made no sound.

Nick leaned against the rail. "Dammit, Catherine! Say something. Anything."

When he looked up she was suddenly there, floating out of the wall of fog. Nick's hands jerked with the instinct to open his arms to her, but he stilled the urge, and she stopped a few feet away from him.

"This isn't the make-believe world of movies," she said. "This is real life and it's filled with real people and real emotions."

"No one is more aware of that right now than I am. Trust me, if this was a movie, I'd edit out this scene fast."

A bright light flickered to life on the point and as the searching beam passed over them, Catherine gasped. "Nick! Your face!"

"Yeah, what about it?"

"When the light flashed I saw a long red welt." She gingerly touched his left cheek. "Right here."

He drew in a sharp breath. "It's nothing."

"What happened?"

"That's a hell of a place to put a potted palm. Anyone stumbling around in the dark could run into it, and those damn fronds are sharp. They can really slice you open if you catch one just right."

"Oh, Nick, I'm sorry," she said, placing her hand over her mouth to hide her teasing smile.

Nick laughed too. "Yeah, I know. It's my own fault for breaking in like I did."

Her eyes widened. "You broke into my apartment? I thought, I mean...well, I just assumed that Henri had let you in and had forgotten to tell me."

"No. I sort of let myself in."

She shook her head. "I suppose it would have been too much for you to just walk back into the restaurant like a normal human being?"

"It would have been easier," he said, then touched his cheek, "and a lot less painful, but there were so many people in there. I decided to wait here until you closed up."

"So I did see something when I came in."

He nodded and grinned again. "It didn't occur to me that you would have Sidney with you." Throwing his hands up, he began to move back and forth. "I couldn't face him twice in one day." Suddenly he stopped and looked up. "Who could?"

Catherine gave a deep throaty laugh.

"You have a sexy laugh," he said, then cursed himself for not keeping their conversation impersonal.

"Thank you," she said, lowering her lashes in shyness.

And that was even sexier, he thought. Damn! It was time to leave before he forgot again who she was. He turned. "Sorry, I don't know why I came back here. I should be going."

"No!" she said, anxiously. "You can't leave yet."

He stopped and faced her. "Why not?"

"Because," she said, refusing to meet his stare. "Well, because...the fog! It's too dangerous to drive in this fog."

He started away again. "I'll manage. I've done it lots of times."

"But I don't want you to go," Catherine said, taking a step toward him, then stopping with her hand still outstretched.

Nick walked back to her. She wouldn't look up at him, so he bent his knees and brought his face down even with hers. "Why, Catherine?"

"You came back to talk," she answered, meeting his gaze with her pleading green eyes, "and we haven't yet. Talked, that is."

He straightened and reached out to touch a curl at the side of her face. He smoothed it back behind her ear as he held her gaze with his. Why did she tug so at his heart? What was it about her?

The searchlight rushed over them again, breaking the spell.

"You haven't asked me anything about Gideon," she said.

An ache from deep within froze his hand at her cheek. "No. No, I haven't, yet." His hand fell to his side. "I'm sure both of us know a lot about him in very different ways, and we should share some of it with each other."

She nodded. "I thought it might hurt both of us less if we talked about him."

Nick drew in a deep breath and moved away. "Sidney's right, isn't he?"

"Sidney? About what?"

He stared into the bleak gray night. "I heard your whole conversation."

She shrugged. "It's not nice to eavesdrop, you know."

He turned and faced her. "You're avoiding the subject."

"I honestly don't know what you're talking about."

"You're wasting away out here. You're hiding from the real world, trying to keep Gideon alive."

She pulled herself taller. "Sidney didn't say that."

"He wanted to, but he was too afraid of making you mad."

"You, on the other hand, aren't?"

"No," Nick answered flatly.

"Well, you're both wrong," she said, as a mask of indifference fell into place. "I live here because this is my home, my work, my life."

Nick decided to drop the subject for the time. "I stand corrected."

She nodded, then turned and started away.

"Where are you going?" he asked.

"To get something to put on that scratch before it gets infected."

"That's not necessary," Nick said, but she was already disappearing behind the silvery curtain of fog. "Catherine!"

There was no reply.

"Come back here!" he ordered.

The deep horn sounded again as an unpleasant reminder of how easily someone could get lost in the dangerously dense fog. "Women," he muttered, leaving the warm pocket their bodies had created.

In the cold damp fog Nick felt like a blind man who'd been thrown into unfamiliar surroundings. His hands groped at nothingness. Damn independent woman, he thought. I'm worried she'll walk off into the ocean, and it'll probably be me instead.

An unexpected breeze blew past him and he turned to follow. A fragrant trail of amber and myrrh led Nick through the earthbound cloud until he came up behind her.

He stopped at a point where he could barely see her shadowy form in the dimness. She was looking for him, and as she turned slowly, the circling light returned to illuminate the area. Her pure white dress glistened for a moment like sparkling snow, but as the beam embraced her fully, the material became almost transparent.

Seeing the rounded curves of her body caused a sudden tightening inside him. As he tried to control his wild inner yearnings Nick wondered why he could not see her for what she was, a link to his best friend and nothing more.

"Oh, there you are," she said, facing him.

The light raced on, and they were left again in darkness, a cover Nick was thankful for. He forced himself to sound joking as he indicated the assortment of packages in her hands. "Damn, woman, did you bring the whole medicine cabinet with you?"

"I couldn't decide which was best, so I brought everything." She turned around and deposited the bottles on something just out of his range of vision.

"Can you see in this pea soup?"

"No, but I know where things are on the deck. Now sit down in that chaise lounge, and let me get a better look at the damage my plant did."

He looked around and saw a padded lounge chair he hadn't noticed before. "This is totally unnecessary, you know. It's just a little scrape."

She poured liquid from a bottle onto a small cotton pad, then turned his face for a better view.

"Don't touch it," he ordered.

"It looks deep."

"It isn't. Leave it alone."

Her hand inched closer to the wound. Nick reached up, grabbing her wrist. "I said, don't touch it." He meant to intimidate her, but his plan failed the instant their eyes met. She was beautiful, though not in the Hollywood sense, but she had the type of beauty that would make a man thankful when he awoke and saw her beside him.

With startling clarity, he remembered how lovely Catherine had looked when she had come to him out of the mist, like something out of a dream. Nick rarely indulged in fantasies, but for one brief moment, he allowed himself to dream of how it might have been if he had met her in another time, another place.

Reality claimed the moment and the vision shattered. Catherine was not his to dream about. She had been Gideon's dream, Gideon's wife. He had no right to think of her as anything else.

He let go of her wrist and stared into the fog.

Her touch was gentle as she dabbed at the scratch, but he yelled anyway.

"Oh, hush," she said.

"Were you this bossy with Gideon?"

She stopped and composed herself before answering. Her voice was tight, restrained. "When I had to be. He was about as good a patient as you are."

"Geez," Nick complained. "That stuff stinks. It smells like a damn hospital out here. I hate hospitals."

"Me, too. Now turn your head just a little."

"I hope Gideon didn't have to spend a lot of time in the hospital. I know how he hated to be confined."

He saw her body tense and she bit her lip before answering. "No. I kept him home as much as possible." She stepped back. "There, I'm finished."

Nick stared at her. "Then it was an illness, not an accident or something?"

Catherine nodded. "Cancer."

It felt as though everything inside Nick ceased to function and he, himself, stopped living for a second. "Oh, my God," he mumbled, dropping his head into his hands.

"They discovered it when he broke his arm on your last job together."

Nick looked up. "You mean he knew it when I left?"

"Yes."

"Well, I thought they kept him in the hospital an awfully long time for just a broken arm, but I knew he was run down and figured he just needed the rest. I had no idea—I mean, he didn't let on that anything... My God. That's why he decided to retire."

"He knew even if the surgery and the chemo worked, he would probably never want to go back to that type of lifestyle." Catherine sat on the foot of the chaise lounge. "So he bought this restaurant and hired me to manage it."

"But when did he have the surgery? How could I have not known?"

"When you decided his retirement was a good time to take that round-the-world sail that you'd always dreamed of, Gideon told the doctors to wait until you'd left."

"That fool," Nick said as every memory of that time came back to him with amazing clarity. "That's why he helped me leave so fast. I mean, I got to see this restaurant only once, and he was saying he was going to be too busy remodeling and everything, so bam!"

Nick remembered Gideon's words exactly. "So take off, O'Donovan. What's the use of hanging around here? I'll just put a hammer in your hand and see how good a carpenter you are."

Nick tilted his head back and looked up at the sky angrily. "Damn, I should have known something was up. I should have stayed."

"He didn't want you to stay. He didn't want you to know, he didn't want anyone to know."

"Why?"

"Would you?"

Nick turned to face her. "No," he finally said.

"Gideon decided to hire a manager for the restaurant and let the manager oversee the remodeling and act as a go-between with his friends."

"I don't understand. Why did he buy this damn place, and remodel it and all, in the middle of...of..."

"He needed something to cling to, something to keep his mind occupied. He figured he'd hire a stranger, someone who had no ties to him, and it would be easier to tell a stranger that he was sick and possibly...going to die."

Nick shook his head. "I can't imagine him hiring you as that stranger."

"Well, he didn't intend to, but I was desperate for a job at the time. My money was running out. I had to find something that week or go back to Oklahoma and my folks. So I just barged in here. It wasn't hard, the whole place was being rebuilt and he was standing in the middle of lumber and Sheetrock."

"And the instant he saw you he hired you."

"Yes," she said, softly. "How did you guess?"

"Professor Marvel never guesses, he knows," he said.

"What?"

Nick laughed self-consciously. "It's from *The Wizard of Oz.*"

Catherine smiled. "Gideon's favorite movie."

"I swear, he used to quote lines from that until I thought I'd deck him."

"You too, huh?"

They smiled at their shared remembrance. She was such a warm inviting person, Nick thought, momentarily jealous of the relationship she and Gideon must have had.

She looked away and continued. "Gideon didn't even glance at my résumé. We just sort of had this intuitive thing between us. He said he knew I'd be the right one for the job."

Catherine stood and put her hands in the pockets of her skirt as she began pacing. "And I did do a good job. Gideon gave me a free hand with the restaurant, but that wasn't the real job he meant. I had to cover for him while he was in the hospital, with Spencer and his stuntmen buddies, when they'd drop by. The worst one was Sidney. He was beside himself at all the money Gideon was putting into this place, and he kept trying to catch him here. I'd go to the hospital every evening and he'd call Sidney. Lord, Gideon should have been an actor instead of a stuntman. No one suspected a thing."

Nick stood and leaned against the railing. He hated to ask, but he had to know. "So, his surgery wasn't successful?"

"No, quite the opposite. Everything seemed fine. They were almost positive they'd gotten it all. The chemo was an extra precaution. The restaurant was about ready to open and Gideon was feeling so much better. Our friendship and respect had grown to much, much more. Things were going great. Of course the doctors always warn you that it can recur anytime, but if he could make it through the next five years..."

She shook her head. "A year passed. Our business was growing and growing. We had become the newest celebrity haunt. And I was in love with Gideon, hopelessly, and he was in love with me. You know, that type of love where someone is so much a part of you that you want to be with them every minute."

Nick looked up. The fog was becoming wispier, and the moonlight was breaking through in an occasional spot. Catherine was caught in the glowing light, her face glistening with tears.

"No," Nick said, pretending he hadn't seen she was crying, "I've never known a love like that."

"I'm sorry. I hope you do someday."

He shrugged. "I don't want that kind of love."

"I thought everyone did."

"No. It's too consuming. I like my freedom."

"That's sad."

"No, it's not, Catherine," his voice rose in volume, as he shoved away from the rail and walked away from her. "Can you hear what I'm saying? I don't want it. I'm very glad that you and Gideon found what you did in each other, but don't wish that sort of thing on me. It would be a fate worse than death for me."

She walked to the rail and leaned out toward the ocean. "I'm trying to understand, but—"

"Let's drop it, okay?"

Catherine nodded.

He moved back and stood beside her, but faced the house. "So you and Gideon were madly in love, what next?"

"Since everything was going so well, we decided not to wait any longer. We were married at the Wayfarers' Chapel."

"Gideon always loved that place, with all those glass walls looking out over the ocean." Nick folded his hands in front of him and nodded toward the house. "It's a lot like this place."

Catherine's voice was tearful when she spoke. "We'd just gotten back from our honeymoon and one night about a month later, he just collapsed.

Sidney was here and we rushed him to the hospital, but...it was back, and the relapse was worse than the first time."

Nick touched her arm. "Catherine, I—"

She flinched at his touch and pulled away. He started toward her, wanting to comfort her, but not sure how.

"No," she said, rushing far enough away from him that she disappeared into the safety of the fog.

"Catherine, I'm sorry. I know this must be painful to tell. I shouldn't have asked you. I should have asked Sidney or someone."

"I brought him home as soon as I could," she continued. "There was really very little anyone could do for him at that point. I just tried to keep him as comfortable as possible. Pain was a way of life, but he rarely let it show. I hired a private nurse and every evening as the studios were closing, we'd dress him and wheel him to the office door. Then, holding onto me, he'd walk to his stool at the bar and he'd sit there and hold court with all his buddies. It was mostly stuntmen and Spencer at first, but when the others heard of his condition, everyone came by. All the technical people, other directors he'd worked with. Movie stars, lord, the two of you must have doubled for every big star in Hollywood."

"Yes, we certainly did," Nick said, closing his eyes and trying not to picture the scene she was describing.

She sniffed.

"Oh, God, Catherine. You're not crying are you?"

"No."

"Good. I can't stand a crying woman."

"Me, either."

He stared down at his boots. "I mean, you have every right to cry, but I just can't handle that kind of sadness."

"Sadness is too ungrateful," she said in a voice choked with tears.

"I've heard that before, somewhere."

"Jennifer Jones in *Love Is a Many Splendored Thing*, another one of Gideon's favorites. I think it's a beautiful sentiment and I try to live it, but— Oh, Nick, I can't. I miss him too much."

"I'm sure you do," Nick said, his own voice faltering slightly, "but curse or scream or yell. Do anything, but please, don't cry."

"I'm not crying."

"Good," he said, reaching into his vest pocket. Nick pulled out a crumpled handkerchief. "Here," he said, holding the red bandanna out blindly.

"Thank you."

In the quiet that followed Nick battled with himself. For the first time in his adult life, he wanted to give as much as he took, but he knew it would be a mistake. Catherine expected the people in her world to offer as much of themselves as she did. He couldn't give that much.

Then she was there, rushing toward him, tears streaming down her face.

"Oh, God, I knew you were crying."

Pressing her cheek against his chest, Catherine wrapped her arms around his waist. Nick held his arms up and away from her as he stared down at her darkly cascading curls.

"Hold me, Nick. Please! I need someone to hold me."

Chapter Five

Nick wanted to relax and hold her, but he was afraid to move. He was afraid he wouldn't have the strength to let her go again. "Don't do this to me, Catherine. I'm not good with emotion."

She backed away, her whole body shaking with her effort to stop crying. "I'm sorry," she coughed out between gasps for air. "I-I'm not u-usually like this. Really! I hav-haven't cried like this since—since—" suddenly a new set of tears burst from her, "—since the night Gideon di—"

Nick reached out and grabbed her arm. Spreading his legs as he leaned against the rail, he hauled

Catherine to him. She fell against his chest and let the sobs rack through her. Obeying an instinct Nick didn't know he had, his arms surrounded her, and he tried to comfort her with soft soothing words.

He held her tightly with one hand, while his other stroked her long auburn curls. "Shhh," he breathed and gently kissed the top of her head. He had stopped her just as hysteria was about to take over, and he knew she would need several minutes to calm down. He didn't mind. It felt natural holding Catherine in his arms. It was as though she had been made to fit his embrace.

Nick closed his eyes, trying to force his thoughts away from her, but he couldn't keep her face from dancing before him. There was no way to ignore the fact that he was still holding her in his arms. Or that he was breathing the same air as she was, air sweetly scented by her presence.

He shook his head. Try as he might, there was no way he could think of her as merely a person in need of consolation. She was a woman. A woman who colored his every thought. A woman who touched his very soul. A woman who could never be his.

"Nick." She started to lift her head to look at him.

"Don't!" Nick ordered. "Don't move. Don't say anything."

He doubted she understood, but nevertheless she rested her cheek against his chest again and didn't move. Nick wasn't sure he understood either. All he knew was that his honor as a gentleman was on shaky ground at that moment.

She grew calmer and was breathing evenly, but Nick could feel his own breath growing ragged, heated. Again he took her arm, but this time he pushed her away from him.

"I need to go," he said in a hoarse voice.

Catherine's eyes filled with surprise and hurt, but she didn't say anything. She lowered her lashes, and Nick gave a quick nod, taking her action as agreement. He strode to her, took her arm, turned her around, and they started toward the house. She couldn't keep up with Nick's long strides, but he couldn't slow down. If he hesitated, he was lost.

Once they stepped inside, Nick released her, and he continued on to the top of the stairs. Grabbing the banister, he stopped. Without turning to face her, he asked, "Will you be all right here, by yourself?"

She didn't answer.

"Will you be all right, Catherine?"

Still she didn't answer. Nick held his stiff pose a second longer, then finally turned to look at her. She was still standing in front of the patio doors, looking small and frail and helpless. Her hand was at her mouth to stop her lips from quivering. Then he saw her head move slightly.

"Was that a yes?" he asked, praying he could get away before she let loose with a new flood of tears.

She swallowed and her nod was more pronounced, but with just as little conviction.

"Fine," he said, hating himself. With a sigh of disgust, he continued, "I know you don't understand, but I think sorrow is something each person should handle on their own."

She didn't respond.

He started to weaken. "But if you want me to, Catherine, I'll stay."

She shook her head. Nick turned and rushed down the stairs. As his foot struck the last step, he heard her give in to tears again. Walk directly to the door, he told himself. Pretend you didn't hear her. No one would blame you.

"Damn," he swore, grabbing the banister. It shook violently as he pulled himself around. "Damn and double damn," he said, taking the stairs two at a time.

Catherine was clutching the back of a wing chair, and her shoulders were slumped over, heaving with her tears. Nick crossed the room in three strides, and when he touched her she went limp. He caught her in his arms before she fell, then he scooped her up and took her to the bed.

When he placed her on the eyelet comforter, she seemed aware of nothing except her need to let the anguish out. Nick stood watching her for a moment, then finally he shrugged out of his bush vest and grabbed the chair. Pulling it beside the bed, he sat and removed his boots. Then he settled back, trying to find a comfortable position. It had been one hell of a day, and it looked as if it were going to be a very long night.

She cried and cried, and though Nick watched her, he tried to think of other things to keep from actually seeing her, thinking of her. Finally, she cried herself to sleep, and Nick let his mind acknowledge his own exhaustion. Just as he was about to doze off, she screamed.

Nick leapt from the chair and was on the bed in what seemed like one movement, cradling her. In her sleep-drugged mind she was still fighting her nightmare. Nick lay back on the bed, still holding her in his arms.

She clung to him as though she dare not let go. "Gideon?"

"Shhh. It's all right, darlin'. Everything's all right."

"Don't leave me," she pleaded.

He held his breath for a moment as Catherine pressed her body closer to his. "I won't leave you," he answered in a raspy voice. "I promise, I won't leave you."

Nick awoke to a world more beautiful than a dream. The first thing he saw was an open window draped in organdy. The curtains billowed with a breeze so tangy he could taste the salt on his lips. Carried above the breeze, Nick heard the waves hitting the pilings beneath the small pier. It was a soothing noise that reminded him of the sound the open sea had made as it slapped against the sides of the *Dangerous Lady*.

Staring out through the sliding glass door, he noticed the sun was high, edging toward midday. Nick could not remember when he had slept so late. Neither could he recall when he had stayed awake most of the night, but cradling Catherine close to him was a pleasure he had wanted to savor for as long as possible. The last thing he remembered was looking at her as dawn crept into the room.

The fragrance of her perfume clung to the comforter and as he rolled over, it blossomed again. It was a delicate scent that evoked more memories of the night before. He had never wanted a woman as much as he had wanted her, and he had never been that close to a woman without them both taking what they wanted.

He frowned. She would probably never admit it, but he knew that Catherine was just as drawn to him as he was to her. It was all so damned unfair. If they had only met under different circumstances. Rolling over, Nick slammed his fist into the pillow. He was happy that Gideon's final days were filled with love, and yet, for some strange reason, Nick also felt a little jealous.

Slowly he let the bright morning work back into his thoughts, and the smell of strong coffee drifted to him. He lay still for a moment, listening to the orchestration of Catherine's movements in the kitchen below.

There was a rhythmic blend of cabinet doors being slammed, silverware clattering against dishes, and the spray of water on the steel sink. Now and then he heard the intake of air as the refrigerator door was opened and then the exhale as it was sucked shut. The homey symphony was completed with the sizzling sound of bacon frying, an occasional tap of an egg on the rim of a bowl, and the pop of the toaster.

Nick rose and pulled on his bush vest as he realized that for the first time he was experiencing a joy that most men would consider routine. When he was sailing around it was usually to exotic places where women were scarce, at least the type of women who fix bacon and eggs for breakfast. Even when he had been in Hollywood, he had mostly dated starlets who were notorious for not knowing how to cook. Besides, they both usually had a five a.m. call at the studio and no one was in the mood for a nice sit-down breakfast at that hour.

Scooping up his boots, Nick started down the stairs, but he stopped when Catherine came into view. A sense of awe overcame him as he saw her again. It was hard to put his feelings into words—rather like trying to explain how he felt when he watched the sunrise at sea.

Nick sat on the top step and pulled on his hiking boots. He didn't want to draw her attention and was careful not to make any noise. Before he finished tying his laces, there was a knock on the sliding glass door. Catherine's face lit up and she waved to the person to come in.

Nick recognized the leather wing tips the instant they stepped in: Sidney. Then two shapely legs entered and instinctively, Nick leaned down to see who was with him. He smiled, recognizing the bleached blond knockout that Sidney had said he'd hired for her shorthand.

"Hi, Sidney," Catherine said, buttering the toast. She nodded toward his secretary. "Bunny, it's good to see you again. I've got a fresh pot of coffee on, want some?"

"No," Sidney said. "We're in sort of a hurry."

"Oooo," Bunny squealed. "I love what you've done with this place."

Sidney drummed his fingers on the cabinet and gave a quick glance around. "It's always looked this way. She hasn't changed anything since Gideon built it."

"Nevertheless," Bunny said as she cruised around the living area. "I like it."

"Thanks," Catherine said, wiping her hands on her apron. "I'll get those papers." She disappeared into her office. "I'm sorry you had to come all the way out here. I could have brought these to you," she called, then stopped when she reentered the room and saw Sidney studying the meal she was preparing. "I was about to have brunch. Want some?"

"Sure," Bunny said.

"No," Sidney said, glaring at his secretary.

Bunny ignored him and continued walking around the living area, checking out Catherine's decor. "And don't worry about it being a bother for us to drive down here. Sidney's been dying to get out here all morning." She placed her hand to her mouth as though she were about to whisper a secret, but she didn't lower her voice. "He's desperate to know if

Hannibal Smith ever showed back up. I bet he's tried to call you at least a dozen times this morning, but your line was always busy, right Sidney?"

Sidney glanced up. "Is all this food just for you?"

Bunny placed her hand on her hip and tapped the toe of her three-inch high-heeled shoe. "I'm talking to you, Mr. Dinsmore."

"Huh? Oh yes," Sidney said, then to Catherine, "Who were you talking to so long?"

"No one, the phone got knocked off the hook somehow, and I didn't realize it until just a few minutes ago."

Sidney took a set of keys from his breast pocket and jangled them. "I've still got these, so I was wondering if old Hannibal ever showed up? Is that homemade marmalade?"

"Yes," Catherine said, placing the jar close enough for Sidney to inspect. "My chef makes it. Now who is this Hannibal person you're talking about?"

Bunny was scrutinizing a sculpture and talking more to herself than anyone. "An original from the Frankart Studio, 1926. I'm impressed. Yes, yes, I am." Then she smiled at Catherine. "Your friend the stuntman. He did double for Hannibal Smith in *Shrine of Death*, didn't he?"

"Yes," Catherine said, finally remembering. "He and Gideon both did. I forgot that was the character's name."

"Well, I don't see how you could forget something like that." Bunny waved her hand at the absurdity of it all. "I mean when Hannibal, pardon me, when Nick, jumped off that mountain, why, my little heart just stopped for the longest time." Her hand went to her ample bosom. "And then when he landed in the water and all those nasty old crocodiles came after him, well, my heart was just fluttering like you wouldn't believe."

Nick shook his head in disbelief. Bunny was a character. He couldn't believe she hadn't gotten Sidney down the aisle yet. Leaning back with his elbows on the landing, Nick continued to watch the whole scene as though it were a play being performed before him.

Sidney looked from Catherine to Bunny and then back to Catherine. Shaking his head, he explained, "Every month on cable they spotlight a different director. This is Spencer Lord month, so I get to hear this kind of replay every morning."

"You know you love it," Bunny said. "You told me yourself that Spencer was your favorite director."

"I imagine what Sidney said was that Spencer was his favorite client, who happens to be a director," Catherine said.

"So maybe you can tell me, because Sidney won't give me a straight answer. How did Gideon and Nick and Sidney get a piece of the hottest director since the golden days of Hollywood?"

Catherine's smile said she knew the story well. "When Gideon and Nick were just starting out, so was Spencer. He was an unheard-of director at the time he hired them. That was all he could afford, two stuntmen for his entire picture. As usual, about halfway through the filming, they went over their budget. Money was tight, in fact, it was almost non-existent."

"So," Sidney interrupted, "that's where I came in. You see, we—the boys and me, they were my clients—we decided instead of a salary on the film they would take a share of the profits. *The Shrine of Death* turned out to be a phenomenal hit, and as they say, the rest is history."

"It was actually Nick's idea," Catherine corrected sweetly. "He saw Spencer's potential from the very first. They've worked together ever since."

"It was the best deal they ever made. Without it, Gideon probably couldn't have bought a hamburger with his savings, and certainly not a restaurant, and

Nick would have had to swim around the world. I, of course, am the one who managed to parlay that money into their present fortune, and Spencer, seeing what a marvelous job I was doing for Harrington and O'Donovan, hired me also."

Bunny was still standing next to the art deco nude when Sidney noticed the two plates, cups, and silverware. "Are you expecting someone else for brunch?"

"Well, yes, I—"

"My, my, my, Catherine, of all your decorations in here, I do have to say, that is the best." Bunny pointed to the top of the stairs. "And I do mean, the very best."

Think fast, O'Donovan, Nick told himself as he stood. Then, trying to appear casual, he started down the stairs rolling up the sleeves of his shirt.

By the time he reached the bottom step, Bunny was waiting for him. "Why, Nick O'Donovan, as I live and breathe, if you aren't the most handsome thing I've seen in days. Possibly months."

"Bunny," he said with a nod. Then he gave another nod toward the kitchen area. "Sidney. When did you two get here?"

Sidney bristled. "The question is: when did you, O'Donovan?"

Bunny slipped her arm through Nick's and walked beside him toward the kitchen. "Why, Sidney, that's not a very polite question to ask, but—" she giggled "—the answer would be most intriguing."

Nick noticed Catherine's blush and was glad the other two were staring at him. "Not that it's any of your business, Sidney, but I stopped by this morning to get my keys. However, as you know, Catherine didn't have them." He stepped up to Sidney and snatched his keys away. "Thanks, old man."

Nick patted Bunny's hand, then carefully lifted it off his arm and backed away with a slight bow. "Anyway, Catherine and I have been sitting around here talking, and somehow the morning just slipped by."

"Yes," Catherine said, jumping in. "And suddenly we both realized that we hadn't eaten. So I was just whipping up some brunch. Are you sure you two wouldn't like to join us? It won't take a minute for me to scramble up some more eggs."

"Why that would be real nice," Bunny said.

"No," Sidney said, then turned to Nick. "Your phones are already working this morning."

Nick didn't like Sidney's prying, but one look at Catherine and he understood Sidney's jealousy. Turning on his camera smile, Nick said, "That's real nice of you to keep track of things like that for me, Sidney."

"I called your house to see if you had gotten home safely last night. Your housekeeper said you never came in."

"That's right," Nick said.

"You had us all very worried, running off like that."

He shrugged. "Call me irresponsible."

"Don't you think we deserve an explanation?"

Nick shrugged. "About what?"

"Where did you spend the night, O'Donovan?"

"Sidney, please! Not in front of the ladies."

Sidney turned several shades of red and Nick patted his back. "I knew you'd understand. Now why don't you stay awhile? I really have to be going anyway." He grabbed a piece of bacon and bit into it as he headed for the door. "Thanks, Catherine, for letting me use your bathroom to freshen up."

"Oh, anytime," she said, confused. "Do you really have to be going so soon?"

"He's been here all morning," Sidney said, recovering his composure. "If the man says he needs to go, then he needs to go."

"See you around," Nick said, starting out the door.

Catherine rounded the counter. "When?"

Nick stopped. "When what?"

Suddenly shy, she dropped her gaze to the floor. "When will I see you again?"

"Soon," Nick said with a wink. "Real soon."

"Real soon, indeed," Catherine muttered after another nearly sleepless night. She rose from the lounger on her deck and walked back into her bedroom. "It's been three days, O'Donovan, and no one's heard a word from you."

Flopping down on the rumpled bed, she folded her arms across the front of her terry cloth robe and stared at the clock on her bedside table. In two more minutes her alarm would go off, as if she needed it.

Sleep, when it came, was fitful. Since that night when Nick had made her remember it all so clearly, she had had terrible dreams. They were confused, crazy dreams, almost nightmares.

She flipped off the alarm before it sounded and went to the bathroom. After turning on the shower, Catherine removed her robe and the Rams jersey she wore for a nightshirt, but as she hung them up, a feeling of tenderness overcame her. Both the shirt and the robe had been Gideon's. She touched the robe gingerly, then lifted it to her face. Burying her nostrils in the material, Catherine breathed in. It no longer smelled of Gideon, but of her. She had kept everything exactly the same, but nothing felt the same anymore.

She glanced out at the bedroom. Even her dreams were different. She had thought they were all about Gideon, until she woke up with Nick's name on her lips. It made no sense. Nothing made sense anymore.

"No," she said suddenly. "I'm not going to think about any of this anymore. I'll go crazy if I do." She grabbed a washcloth and entered the stall. "Scarlett and I shall think about this tomorrow."

As she showered she forced her mind to concentrate on the next few hours. She would down a glass of orange juice, throw on her sweats and go for a run on the beach. She would run and run and run until she couldn't think, or run anymore.

But as she was ready to go out the door, something stopped her. It was an alternate plan, a plan that had been festering in the back of her mind. Moving back to the kitchen counter, she grabbed the phone and dialed Nick's number. She had it memorized, since she'd called it at least a dozen times over the past three days, but she had always hung up before it started to ring. This time she didn't.

"O'Donovan residence," a woman said in a sleepy voice.

Everything inside Catherine froze for a split second. "Sorry," she finally said, "I must have the wrong number." Hanging up, she told herself she was a fool to call him. For the hundredth time, she reminded herself that her concern for Nick was only because of his closeness to Gideon, but deep inside she knew different. Why else would she have been hurt that a woman answered his phone at six o'clock in the morning?

Glancing around the room, a feeling of emptiness overcame her. A shiver worked up and down her spine. With just his presence Nick had filled her apartment with warmth. More important, he had filled her with warmth. When he was around she felt alive again. Like it or not Catherine had to admit she cared for Nick simply because he was Nick.

"But I don't want to feel that way," she said, pounding her fists on the counter. "Ack!" she yelled. "I've got to get him off my mind."

Hurrying out of the house, Catherine breathed in the crisp morning air. She jogged down the walkway to the steps that led to the beach below. At the bottom of the steps she stopped and began a few warm-up exercises.

"Morning," Nick said, pushing away from a piling he was leaning against. "I was about to give up on you taking a walk today."

Catherine hadn't seen him in the shadows beneath the pier and her heart lurched at the sound of his voice. Looking up, she resisted the urge to run to him. "You know, Nick," she said, trying to sound offhanded. "Once, just once, I wish you'd call or knock or, you know, give a person some warning that you're here."

He shrugged. "I thought I just did."

She placed her foot against the third step and lunged into it to stretch the calf muscle on her other leg. "You're always bursting through doors or breaking in or jumping out of the shadows."

"Sorry, guess it's the stuntman in me. I'm used to making some sort of grand smashing entrance."

Catherine didn't bother to answer, she just glared at him a moment, then took off running.

Nick jogged up beside her. "Something wrong?"

She wanted to give him a quick nasty look, but when she saw that his tall physique was clad only in running shorts and a sweatband, Catherine found it hard to look away. Then she remembered the woman's voice on the telephone, and bitterness edged her voice when she spoke. "I called your house a few minutes ago to see if you were still alive or if you'd fallen off the face of the earth or what."

"I wasn't there."

"No, but she was."

"I see. And this bothered you?"

"Of course not."

"Good, because she's my housekeeper. She is sixty-two and boy, is she going to be mad that someone called and woke her up this early."

Catherine was too mad at herself to speak. His housekeeper! She should have known. Damn. She'd acted like someone petty enough to be jealous, and that wasn't like her at all. Besides, they were supposed to be just friends, and friends don't get jealous.

"Are you mad at me about something?" he asked, breaking the silence.

"What makes you think that?" she snapped, picking up her pace a little.

"It was just a silly thought I had."

"Me? Mad?" she asked, hating the way she was acting and yet unable to stop herself. "Just because you said you'd be in touch soon and then you never call? No, I'm not mad."

"I don't understand. It's only been a couple of days."

"Three days, Nick. Three whole days."

"So?"

"So, I expected to hear from you before now, and then you show up acting like you'd done nothing wrong."

His hands flew up. "I haven't!"

"Oh, forget it, Nick."

"No. I won't forget it. Explain what I've done wrong. I want to try and understand you, Lord knows why, but I do."

"It's just that I take friendships very seriously. I think you have to work at them to keep them alive, to make them grow."

"And three days isn't working at it in your opinion?"

"Right."

Nick ran in front of her, then turned to face her and jogged backwards. "Let me see if I understand this. You think because I didn't call for three measly days that our friendship is in jeopardy."

"Something like that, yeah."

"May I ask you something, then?"

"Sure."

"Catherine, when was the last time you saw or heard from Sidney?"

"Why?"

"Just answer the question."

She didn't want to answer his question, but she had to. "Three days ago," she mumbled.

"I'm sorry, I didn't hear you."

"Three days!"

Nick nodded. "And are we equally upset with him?"

"We're not talking about Sidney, we're talking about you."

"But it makes sense—"

She stopped and dug her heels in the sand. "Don't you dare pull that on me, Nick O'Donovan."

He stopped but continued to run in place. "Don't pull what on you?"

"Logic! If you think you are going to get me to admit to logic when I'm this mad, you're wrong."

"Forgive me, it was a foolish idea."

She finally laughed at herself. "Well, I guess I have been overreacting a little."

"A little?"

"Okay, a lot." She kicked at the sand. "Don't make me feel any worse than I already do."

Nick bent down and smoothed the sand with his hand. Then he sat facing the ocean. Catherine stood awkwardly on one foot and then the other. Finally he patted the spot next to him. "It's for you," he said, then glanced up and down the beach. "There's no one else around."

She sat, clasping her hands around her legs and drawing them close to her chest.

"Catherine, I'd like to be your friend, really, but you're going to have to accept me the way I am."

"And how is that, Nick?"

"A man who says he'll be in touch soon, but puts no timetable on the word soon. Time doesn't matter to me like it does to most people."

"Like sailing away for two years and never even sending a postcard?"

"Exactly! But that doesn't mean I didn't think of Gideon. I wrote him long, long letters when I was at sea. I would just forget to mail them when I reached a port. All I could think of when I'd hit land was getting supplies and sailing off again. And out there, days, weeks, months, even years, don't matter."

"But you're not out there anymore."

"True. I'm back in this so-called world of civilization, and everywhere I turn I have to follow the clock. On certain things, like my job, it's absolutely necessary, but I hate it. That's why I ignore it everywhere else I can. I try to make very few definite plans. I prefer to go where I want, when I want. I guess that's why I'm always just popping in, unexpected."

"I've never known anyone like you before, Nick."

"Nor I, anyone like you."

"What are you talking about? I'm just like everybody else in this civilized world."

"Are you? I doubt it. But then I can't be sure because I've never let myself get close to you normal people before."

"What about Gideon?"

"He didn't care about time either, at least not the Gideon I knew. I suppose by the time you met him, time meant everything to him."

"Yes."

"I hope you'll forgive me, Catherine, but I'm glad I wasn't around to see him have to change."

They were quiet for a moment, each drifting into their own thoughts. Catherine began to realize that for as much as she knew about Gideon, it was all only one side of him. There had been another side to Gideon, a side he had abandoned before she met him, a side Nick knew better than he knew himself.

Suddenly, Nick clapped his hands together and rubbed them briskly. "Well, enough of that kind of talk. Did Spencer ever get a hold of you?"

"About the Stuntmen Awards?"

"Yes. Are you going?"

She nodded.

"Well, then, just for you, I'm going to break my own rule and arrange something two days ahead of time. Would you like to go together?"

Catherine stared at him in stunned silence.

His words rushed out one on top of the other. "I mean, it was just a thought. You know? Since they'll be giving Gideon a posthumous award and all, I just thought, but of course, if you'd rather not. . . ."

"No!"

"That's okay. I understand."

"No. No."

"Okay, Catherine, I heard you. You don't have to be so adamant about it."

"No! I mean, no, I'd not rather not."

Nick's eyes narrowed. "Catherine, this is not that hard. Simply nod your head yes if you would like to go together, or shake your head no if you would not like to go together to the ceremony."

"I'd love to."

"Oh. Good." He stood and smiled. "All right, then, I'll see you Saturday night."

"That's all? You came all the way down here just to ask me that?"

"Yeah. Don't tell me you have something in your rule book on friendship about me asking you things like this in person?"

"Of course not, silly."

"That's a relief."

"I just think it's a shame for you to think you have to leave so soon. Won't you at least let me fix you breakfast? I owe you one anyway."

"Well, that did smell awfully good the other day. . . ."

"Great," she said, standing. "Let's go." They turned and started back to the apartment. "Nick, where's your car?"

He followed her gaze to the front of the pier. "Oh, I didn't drive. I ran down here."

She stopped. "From your house?"

He nodded.

"That's disgusting. You're barely even sweating."

He jogged circles around her. "I have to stay in shape. My job depends on it and I've found running is about the best way to keep me fit."

Catherine started moving again. "Your job?"

"Yeah, stunt work, you know, as in the awards banquet we're going to."

"Of course I know what stunt work is, I just—well, I thought you weren't going to do that anymore."

Nick pulled back. "What ever gave you that idea?"

"The cruise. You were gone two years. I thought you had decided to retire from that type of work, like Gideon."

"Retire! Me? No way. I'd been wanting to sail around the world for years, but there was never enough time between movies. Then, when Gideon said he wanted out, well, it seemed like as good a time as I might get. So, with his encouragement, I took off, but I always intended on returning to work. I've got some incredible new ideas on how I can master some of the old gags that used to give us problems."

"But stunt work is so dangerous."

He laughed. "So is walking across the street."

"But it's like you're taking too many chances. You know, tempting the fates."

"I don't understand. Why are you so upset?"

"I'm not upset," she said, angrily.

"You could have fooled me."

He was right, she was upset, but she hadn't realized why until that moment. "I just don't understand why you want to keep taking such chances. You could get hurt."

"That's why they pay me so well," he said with a laugh.

Catherine didn't laugh. It was too serious a subject to joke about. She had lost one man she loved, and she couldn't face the thought of losing another. Of course she didn't love Nick, she told herself. She had known him less than a week. She had, however, grown very fond of him in that short time, and the thought of the misery that one miscalculation could cause made her shiver.

"Nick, you're risking your life every time you do one of those gags."

Nick stopped and pointed to himself. "But it's my life, Catherine, and I'm the only one who has to answer for it."

She stopped, too, her hand on her hip as she faced him. "Oh, I see, you're a free agent, so to speak?"

"Right," he said, as though the argument should end there.

"And hang your responsibility to others."

The look in his eyes told Catherine that he had engaged his defense again. "The only responsibility I have is to myself."

"No man is an island, what one person does will somehow affect others, especially his family and friends."

"I have no family, and if this conversation is an example of what it's like to have friends, I understand why I have very few."

"And I understand why you don't have many friends, if you're always this selfish."

"Me? Selfish? What about you? You're asking me to change my whole life style."

"You were the one spouting logic a minute ago." She shrugged. "I'm just giving you a taste of your own medicine."

"This is logic?"

"Yes."

Nick brought the back of his hand down into the palm of his other hand. "Catherine, it is not logical for a man to give up his livelihood."

"Sidney's invested your money wisely enough, you don't have to go right back to work. You could take this time to reevaluate your life and try something different."

"Why? I'm perfectly happy with my life exactly the way it is."

"There's a million things you could do."

"Like what, buy a restaurant?"

"Well, I was thinking of other jobs in the industry, but yes, a restaurant wouldn't be a bad idea."

He threw his hands up and began pacing in a small circle. "It would be the worst idea. You might as well slit my wrists than to wish that type of life on me."

"Nick, I'm not trying to ruin your life. I'm only trying to make you see that there are other ways of making a living that aren't life threatening."

He stopped and looked up at her. "Oh, I get it. This is like the other morning on the beach when you jumped in after me."

She considered the analogy a moment, then nodded in agreement.

"Catherine, I want you to listen very closely to what I'm about to say. I wasn't drowning then, and I'm not drowning now. Quit trying to save me."

She glared at him. "Okay! Go ahead. Get yourself killed, see if I care."

He opened his mouth to speak, but Catherine cut him off. "And another thing. You can forget Saturday night. I wouldn't go with you if you were the last man on earth."

Nick threw his head back as he rolled his eyes. "Oh, that was very original. But don't worry," he said, backing away. "I withdraw the offer anyway."

Catherine turned and faced the ocean. "Don't bother, I refuse the offer."

He held out his forefinger and jabbed the space between them. "You can't refuse it if I withdraw it."

She folded her arms across her chest. "I can and I will." She glanced over her shoulder and sneered. "So there."

"Women!"

"Boys," she said, facing the water again.

"Oh, that was low, Catherine. Really low."

"I can get lower."

"Never mind, I'm leaving."

"Good!" she called after him. "And if I never see you again, it'll be too soon!"

"That goes double—no," he said, then paused in his retreat and threw his final words with his outstretched arm, "that goes triple for me."

Chapter Six

There was not a doubt in Catherine's mind that it was the worst evening of her life. The presentation of awards seemed to go on forever. Damn Nick O'Donovan, she thought, he had ruined the ceremony for her. She stared across the circular table. Just look at him, she fumed, he's having a great time, and I'm over here miserable.

At the podium, two of Hollywood's favorite leading men were staging a childish, comic debate: "My stuntman's better than your stuntman." Catherine was only half listening, as she had done most of the night. Every time they would lower a screen on the stage and show a clip of a spectacular stunt, she would find her mind drifting off. Without fail she would begin to picture Nick performing the stunt, but in her mind's eye, he never emerged unscathed. Something always went wrong, and she would experience the terror of seeing him bruised and battered or burned and broken.

And, also without fail, she would be rudely pulled back into reality by the high-pitched giggle of Nick's date. Catherine cursed her lack of foresight not to realize that, even if she went with someone else, Spencer would still expect her to sit at his table with his other honored guest, Nick.

So there they all sat, Catherine and her date, Sidney, and Nick with Bunny, his date, and of course, Spencer, who, being too absorbed in his work, forgot to get a date. They hadn't seen much of the young director though, as he had spent most of his time hopping up and down to check on things backstage. He said it was because he was coordinating the event, which he was, but Catherine suspected Spencer was trying to escape the murderous looks that were being flung around his table.

Out of the corner of her eye Catherine watched the overly happy couple across from her. Bunny was in rare form: she laughed too loudly, batted her eyes too often and clung too desperately to Nick's arm. She demanded his full attention and got it, along with the attention of half the other men in the room. Her bimbo act put Marilyn Monroe's best performance to shame.

And her dress! Catherine had felt like a Pollyanna in her simple black crepe when she saw Bunny's hot pink sheath. Catherine had managed to hide her own amazement, but Sidney had no poker face. He had stared, openmouthed, at the generous cleavage revealed by the bias cut of Bunny's strapless gown. Although there had never been any doubt about Bunny's assets, that night she was displaying them with pride.

Then there was Nick. Catherine couldn't keep her eyes off him. He looked both elegant and casual in his cutaway tuxedo and western tie. She smiled, remembering that Sidney had said it was the first time that he had seen Nick when he didn't look as if he were in a cigarette ad. Catherine knew that Nick preferred his rugged he-man style of life, but the manner in which he wore sophistication reminded her that he had once fit easily in the glittering world of Hollywood.

He had been compelling before, but now, after he'd shaved his beard, irresistibly handsome were the only words that came to mind. He glanced up and caught her staring. With a sly smile he lifted his wineglass in salute.

She wanted to die, but held her composure and gave him a bored look, then glanced back at the stage. Catherine tried to concentrate on the award being handed out for best action sequence, but she could feel Nick staring at her, and she was growing warmer by the moment.

Suddenly, Spencer was there beside her, leaning down with a worried expression on his face.

"What's wrong?" Catherine whispered.

Spencer offered a big smile and spoke softly through clenched teeth. "Aren't you supposed to be somewhere right now?"

"No," Catherine answered, while wishing she *was* somewhere else, anywhere that Nick wasn't.

"We were just leaving," Nick whispered, standing and coming around the table. He pulled Catherine's chair out for her. "Let's go."

She didn't stand. "Let's not," Catherine said, without standing. "I'm not going anywhere with you, O'Donovan."

"Oh, yes you are," Nick said, a teasing, but serious lilt to his voice.

"Oh, no I'm not," she answered.

"Oh, yes you are," Spencer said, taking her by one arm and lifting her from the chair.

Nick took her other arm and the threesome headed toward the stage door.

"What's going on here?" Catherine demanded, in a low hostile voice.

"Your cue was four minutes ago," Spencer said, not looking at either of them, but nodding and waving to people in the audience.

"What cue?" Catherine asked, looking first at one man and then at the other.

Spencer glanced at her. "Don't you remember anything from the rehearsal, Catherine?"

"Rehearsal? The last rehearsal I went to was when our high school did *Annie Get Your Gun*, and that was ten years ago."

Spencer finally let his gaze meet hers. "You didn't come with Nick this afternoon?"

"Was I supposed to?"

Spencer looked past Catherine and offered Nick a lethal grin. "Nick, what's going on here? You told me the other day that the two of you would accept this award for Gideon, and that both of you would go to the technical run-through this afternoon."

Nick said hello to a table of fellow stuntmen, then without looking at Spencer or Catherine, he replied offhandedly, "Catherine and I aren't speaking to each other at the moment."

As they entered the backstage area, Spencer's smile disappeared instantly and his angry director look took its place. "Are you trying to tell me that in exactly three and one half minutes you two are going to step out on that stage, and neither of you knows what you're supposed to do?"

Nick gave him a patronizing look. "Don't worry. I was at the rehearsal today. I know what to say and do."

"You'd better," Spencer said, leaving them in the wing left of the stage.

Without Spencer at her side, Catherine jerked free of Nick's hold. "And what about me? Were you just going to let me stand out there gawking like a complete idiot?"

"You'll do fine," Nick said.

"Damned right I will, because I won't be there. I'm going back to my seat." She turned and started away.

"You can't do that," Nick said, grabbing her arm.

"Hide and watch," she snapped, trying to release herself from him.

"Catherine, I don't blame you for being mad at me, but you've got to be there. It's for Gideon."

She lost her will to fight. He was right, she had to do it. "You knew you had the trump card all along, didn't you?"

"I was wrong, I should have told you earlier about the rehearsal."

"Nick, you never told me at all. Spencer did, a few minutes ago."

"I tried to call you, but you weren't in."

"When?"

"This morning."

"I was home until noon."

"Okay, so I didn't call until this afternoon. At least I did finally call."

"And what about the past couple of days? Didn't it occur to you to give me a little advance notice, or is that making plans too far ahead of time?"

"I wanted to call, but I... I was too scared."

She raised an eyebrow. "Nick O'Donovan, scared? I find that hard to believe."

"You find it hard to believe! I was astounded. I mean, hell, I can face two grizzly bears alone in the Alaskan wilderness. But calling you? After the things we'd said? I just couldn't bring myself to do it."

She looked at him, wanting to believe him, but afraid to believe him. "Oh, sure, you'll say anything to get me out on that stage, won't you?"

Just then the emcee said Gideon's name. They both froze, listening and watching. Again the screen descended to the stage, and Gideon's face was projected, five feet tall. The film proceeded with a beautiful tribute in words and action. His most famous stunts were panned, but the touching parts were the outtakes, and an assortment of rare footage from the early days of Harrington and O'Donovan.

Catherine recognized Spencer Lord's touch. He had composed the video with loving care, and Catherine doubted she was the only one with tears in her eyes. The voice-over was a raspy rough voice with just a slight hint of vulnerability. It was Nick's voice. Catherine looked up at him. The pain was evident on his face, and she realized how hard it must have been for him to have worked on the piece with Spencer.

As the video ended to thundering applause, Nick put his arm around Catherine's waist. "I knew you'd be too choked up to talk, so just say thank you and I'll do the rest."

She nodded, glad she had him to lean on.

"Try not to think about the cameras that are taping this for a delayed broadcast on cable."

"Thanks for reminding me," she said, almost laughing.

Nick smiled at her. "That's my girl. Now relax. Everything will be fine."

"And this from a man who's admitted he can't handle dialogue."

But Nick was right, everything came off without a hitch. His acceptance speech was brief and filled with the type of emotion that men understand. It was the type of emotion that touched the other stuntmen in a way Catherine wouldn't have expected. It touched her, too. For a brief moment, while she clutched the award to her breast and listened, she felt she finally understood the unique brotherhood that exists among the men who place their lives in jeopardy every day.

She began to wonder if she had overreacted to Nick's announcement that he was going back to work. All the men she'd seen there that night appeared to be in the best of health. They kept themselves in top physical condition and from hearing Gideon talk, she knew that they always took every precaution in their work.

When Nick was through, he stepped back, and Catherine moved to the microphone. "Thank you, for Gideon. I know this would make him very proud." Then Nick placed his hand at the small of her back and escorted her offstage.

In the darkened wing, Catherine stopped and looked up at Nick. "Maybe I was wrong."

He started taking off his jacket. "About what?"

"Well, maybe knowing a stuntman isn't any worse than having a friend who is a fireman or a policeman. I mean, they take chances with their jobs too."

He was in the process of loosening his tie, and he stopped to look at her. "I'm glad you feel that way because—"

"Nick," Spencer called in an overwrought voice. "Quit standing around talking. We've got a show to put on here."

Suddenly there were nine men surrounding Nick and scooting Catherine out of the way. Stunned, she moved aside and watched dozens of hands pulling and tugging on Nick's clothes. Once they had stripped him to his shorts, some of the men rushed away. One man tossed Nick a gauzy-looking body stocking and he began to pull it on. Then the other men were back, carrying buckets that were frosted on the outside and full of an odd-looking gel.

As they began to smear the gel all over Nick's body stocking, Catherine had to ask, "What on earth are they doing to you?"

Nick peered over the heads of the men and winked. "I'm taking out the envelope in a minute."

Catherine nodded. When it was time for the envelope with the name of the winner, she'd heard, one of the stuntmen would arrive on stage simulating the type of stunt it was for.

As they began applying the gel to Nick's hair, Catherine shook her head. "Will that stuff come out?"

"With a lot of scrubbing," Nick laughed.

"And just how are you going to present the envelope?" she asked.

Spencer suddenly appeared again with a strange-looking bodysuit. "Er, Catherine, watch out behind you. Why don't you move over there? That guy is mixing napalm, and I don't want you near it." Then he smiled at Nick. "Ready to suit up?"

"Napalm?" Catherine asked in a squeaky voice. "Napalm, as in napalm bomb?"

Spencer was helping Nick into the suit, and he glanced back at Catherine. "Yes, I guess. It's an explosive, if that's what you're asking."

Appalled, Catherine looked up at Nick, but one of the men was pulling a cap over his head and face. "Spencer Lord, I demand you tell me what you're doing right now!"

Spencer blinked. "I thought it was obvious. We're going to set Nick on fire."

"What?" Catherine almost shouted, rushing up to Nick. "Are you really going through with this?"

Spencer took her hand and moved her out of the way of the men who were now rubbing the gel over the top of the suit. "He can't hear you," Spencer said. "Once they put that cap on he's deaf and blind. In fact, he can't even tell when he's been set on fire. I have to signal him with my hand on his back."

"My God, Spencer, what if something goes wrong and he can't tell you?"

"He has a hand signal he'll give and I'll watch for it from the moment he's ignited."

Catherine felt too weak to speak.

"Relax," Spencer said. "This gel has been kept near freezing, it's an amazing protector. See, first we rub it on the body stocking, then on this outer suit, which is made of this new fireproof material, then we put regular clothes on over that and set them on fire."

"Can Nick breathe in there?"

"Sure. At least until we set him off."

"What?"

"Catherine, didn't Gideon ever discuss this stuff with you?"

"Not in detail."

Spencer ran his fingers through his thick black hair. "I can see why, but don't worry so much. Didn't you see the compressed air bottle inside of the fireproof suit? We wait until the last second before he's lit and turn it on for him. He has a three minute supply of air and it keeps him safe from the toxic gases and stuff like that."

"Stand by," one of the men said.

They all moved away to reveal what must have been Nick, but to Catherine it looked like a mummy dressed in a business suit. Spencer and two of the men led Nick to his entrance point, while everyone else grabbed a fire extinguisher and followed. Catherine wished she had oxygen to help her breathe as she watched the man with the napalm bucket begin to carefully apply the explosive to Nick's sleeves and legs.

With an amazing precision the napalm man stepped back, another man flipped on Nick's air, and a third man used a cigarette lighter to ignite him. Spencer gave Nick the signal simultaneous to the announcer asking for the envelope.

A human torch staggered onto the stage, and the sound system played a tape of someone screaming in agony. On cue, Nick fell to the ground and the men surrounded him, spraying him with foam. Within seconds the fire was out, and they were hauling Nick to his feet. Someone pulled off his headgear, and Nick smiled, giving the okay signal. They unzipped his charred suit and he reached inside, withdrew an envelope and handed it to the announcer. The crowd went wild as Catherine slumped against the beaming director. "Great take," Spencer said.

The next half-hour was total confusion. Due to the messy ending of Nick's stunt, it was the last award of the night. Spencer gave his closing remarks, the credits rolled and the auditorium gave a collective sigh of relief as the bright lights were turned off. Nick was taken to the shower, and by the time Catherine made it out of the backstage area the entire room was buzzing with conversation and congratulations. It was a minglers heaven and Catherine spotted Sidney doing just that.

Everyone had a comment about Gideon or Nick or both, and Catherine tried not to appear rude as she acknowledged them and bullied her way through the crowd to reach Sidney.

"Oh, there you are," Sidney said, as she touched his arm. "We were just talking about Nick's stunt." He indicated the two men with him. "Wasn't it wonderful?"

"Peachy," she said. "Er, Sidney, can we go?"

"You mean, go, as in home? Leave?"

"Yes, this has been a very trying night. I'm exhausted." And, she thought to herself, she wanted to get away before Nick came back out. His stunt had petrified her, and she had finally realized how deeply she cared about him. All hope of friendship was gone. She was falling in love with Nick O'Donovan.

"All right, we'll leave in a few minutes," Sidney said, patting her hand. Then he leaned closer. "First I've got to make as many contacts as possible."

She glared up at him. "This is a date, not a business proposition. I'm the only person you're supposed to mingle with."

"And I will—later." He gave her a complimentary peck on the cheek, then turned back to the men he had been talking with.

Catherine stood beside Sidney, a smile pasted on her face, although she was surprised no one could see the steam coming out of her ears. She didn't know if she was more mad at Sidney or Nick or herself. How could it have happened? How could she have let herself fall for Nick?

She honestly had never expected to fall in love again. Even in her wildest imagining, Catherine had thought if she ever had a deep relationship with anyone again, it would be more as friends, not lovers. With Gideon it had grown over months, a gentle love filled with respect and admiration; sort of a quiet awakening. But Nick! Everything about him was explosive, and when she was with him, she felt charged, too. A look, a touch, a kiss, they were all filled with passion and fireworks—and confusion.

"Sidney," she finally said, tugging on his sleeve, "I want to leave. Now!"

But it was too late, the voices of the others came drifting to her.

"Way to go, O'Donovan."

"You were really hot tonight."

"I see you haven't lost your touch, O'Donovan."

"Hey, Nick, do you always get so fired up at these things?"

Catherine took a deep breath and prepared herself to face him. She could see him working his way toward her and Sidney. He had a strange look on his face, and Catherine was afraid for a split second that he knew what she was feeling for him.

Their eyes were locked on each other across the distance between them. Both were only vaguely aware that anyone else was in the room. It was as if they were caught in a hypnotic trance that was pulling them together.

Then Bunny was there, stepping between them. Her voice and presence broke the spell, and Nick was pulled away with only a fleeting glance over his shoulder. Catherine sighed with relief. She had to get out of there, she simply had to.

It was wrong, she told herself. What she was feeling for Nick was all wrong. She had once been in love with a very wonderful man. That type of love only comes along once in a lifetime. What she felt for Nick had to be just physical. That was all. It was just as Sidney had said—she was too vulnerable right now, and Nick just happened to be there.

Catherine didn't bother to ask this time, she just released Sidney's arm and walked back to their table. If she didn't get out of there something was going to happen that she didn't want to happen. As she gathered her shawl and clutch purse, Sidney came huffing up to the table.

"What are you doing?"

She glanced up. "I told you. I want to go."

"But I've got those two guys eating out of the palm of my hand. Just a few more minutes and I'll have them as clients."

"Go on back, Sidney. Sign them up. Talk tax shelters and high-yielding mutual funds to your heart's content. I'm taking a cab home."

"But you can't," Sidney whined.

"No, you can't," Nick said, behind Catherine.

She whirled around to face him, then regretted her action. Lifting her chin in false courage, she asked, "And why not? Will I miss them shooting you out of a cannon or something?"

Again, Bunny's shrill voice interrupted them. "No, silly." She wrapped herself around Nick's arm. "Haven't you heard Nicky's plan?"

"Nicky?" Catherine asked.

Nick shrugged.

Bunny wiggled and flipped her hand at Catherine and Sidney. "Oh, it's just marvelous. You'll love it."

Spencer came up, patting Nick's back. "What great fun, Nick. What made you think of it?"

Nick shrugged again. "I don't know. Everything seemed to be dying down here and I thought, hey, why not liven things up a bit?"

Spencer checked his watch. "How long have we got until closing?"

"About twenty-five minutes," Bunny said. "We'd better hurry."

"What's closing?" Sidney asked. "Where do we need to hurry to?"

Spencer laughed. "I don't know how it came up, but somebody said something about amusement parks and the next thing you know, Nick here is suggesting we all go make the last ride on the big old merry-go-round at Griffith Park. Isn't that wild?"

Nick grinned. "It was just a thought, but everyone seems to love it."

"The caravan's leaving in five minutes," someone called from the doorway.

"Wait for me!" Spencer hollered. He hurried past Catherine. "I feel like a kid again."

"So," Nick asked as the foursome again were left alone, staring at each other. "Are you two coming?"

"You can't be serious," Sidney said. "How do you think it would look for a man in my position to do something like that?"

Catherine didn't want to be in the same city as Nick, much less in the same park, but Sidney's attitude changed her mind. "Oh, come on. It'll be fun. I haven't done anything like that in years."

He frowned. "I've never done anything like that." Then he saw the two men he'd been talking with earlier leaving with Spencer. "Then again, maybe we should give this a try."

"That's what I love about you, Sidney. You're such an impetuous silly fool," Nick said, as they all headed for the door.

"Just how rich are those two guys?" Catherine asked.

"Rich enough to get me on a merry-go-round."

The caravan consisted of five cars, three limos and a van, so Catherine was as surprised as the carousel operator when thirty-five formally dressed people showed up at the huge 1926 Spillman.

The crowd was as giddy as a group of teenagers as they began mounting their steeds. Catherine hurried toward the inside rim. She grabbed the reins of an Arabian and a stallion and motioned for Sidney to join her.

He held up his hand and shook his head. "I'm not climbing up on one of those things. What do I look like, John Wayne or something?"

She spread her legs and placed her hand on her hip. "What are you intending to do, stand beside me and hold my hand like my mother used to?"

"See here, Catherine, that was uncalled for. It just so happens there is a marvelous seat right up there." He pointed past a couple of rows of horses.

"That's for grandmothers and nannies."

"No, it's not. It's for lovers. Look how high the back and sides are. It was tailor-made for cuddling."

Catherine's reply was stopped by Bunny's high-pitched, "Yoo-hoo."

Sidney looked up and smiled. He wiggled his fingers in a coy wave and yoo-hooed back.

"We've been looking all over for you," Bunny called, dragging Nick along beside her.

Catherine turned her back to them. She lifted the full skirt of her long dress and placed her foot in the stirrup. The horse had been stopped high on the rod, and she stood for a second debating how to seat herself gracefully. Suddenly she was lifted onto the Arabian's back and deposited sidesaddle.

"Thank you, Sid..." Her voice trailed off as she glanced down into Nick's dark brown eyes.

He smiled up at her. It was a dazzling smile that made her heart sing. The charade was over, and she could tell by the look in his eyes that he knew something had happened inside her. With a single look he had woven a spell that turned the night into something mystical.

Bunny's giggle intruded harshly on her thoughts, and Catherine frowned, but when she looked around there was no one close but Nick. "Where's Sidney and Bunny?"

"It sounds like they're having a grand time in the sissy seat." He indicated the carved gondola three rows ahead of them. "It appears we've both been abandoned. Mind if I ride beside you? I promise, no trick riding."

"Nick I—"

He held up his hand. "Don't say it. When we talk, all the wrong things are said, so let's just enjoy this moment of fantasy."

The operator released the switch and the machinery gave a low moan. The wooden platform creaked in place a moment, then slowly began to move. Nick swung onto the stallion in a long graceful movement.

As their horses pranced up and down, a tune whistled from the shiny pipes of the calliope and Nick sang along. Catherine studied the expression she had not been able to see when he had had his beard. Now she could see the sexy laugh lines at the side of his mouth, and the full sensuousness of his lips was more evident.

Catherine felt as though she were a butterfly emerging from a gauzy cocoon. Everything looked new and fresh again. As the world swirled around them in a blur of brightly colored lights, yesterday and tomorrow did not matter. Even today was lost. They were suspended in a time where nothing could go backward or forward, only around and around and around.

Sadly, the fantasy started to fade. With another creak and groan from the ancient contraption, they began to slow down. The turntable seemed almost as reluctant to end the ride as those on board, but finally it stopped. Nick dismounted as though he was doubling in a B-Western, but when he stepped in front of her to help her down, he had the look of a gallant knight.

Catherine leaned forward and placed her hands on his shoulders as his hands circled her waist. He lifted her off the Arabian and held her in midair until she looked down into his eyes. Slowly, deliberately, he lowered her. Their bodies brushed against each other, bringing an awareness to them that could not be denied.

Finally her feet touched the platform, but the embrace of their gaze made her feel as though she were still suspended. She wished the moment could last forever, and as she stared into his eyes, Catherine felt it might. He placed his fingers beneath her chin and lifted her face as he bent forward.

Everything inside her told her to grab the brass ring and forget about the repercussions. Never mind that she was someone else's date. Never mind that Nick had been Gideon's best friend. Never mind that loving him would mean wondering and worrying every minute that he might not survive his next stunt.

She drew back from his kiss. The hurt that lined his face made her own pain twice as deep. Beneath the daring exterior was a gentle man who was as afraid of rejected love as anyone. Catherine reached up and touched his cheek. "I'm sorry, Nick."

He grabbed her hand and moved it away. "I'm sorry too, Catherine. I'm sorry we'll never see each other again." With that, he turned and strode away. And whether it was pride or pain that kept his shoulders straight, Catherine didn't know.

All she knew was that the ride had ended.

Chapter Seven

Catherine sat, still in her formal gown, on her redwood deck, which extended over the ocean. It was almost dawn and she had done nothing since Sidney had brought her home but sit and think. No matter how, or what she labeled her feelings, she always came up with the same truth: she was falling in love with Nick.

"Falling?" she questioned aloud. "Try fallen, Catherine. You've already fallen in love with him."

Staring down at her lap, Catherine wondered how she could have been so naive as to have thought that she would honestly never be attracted to another man. She absently played with a fold in the skirt of her dress. But he wasn't just another man, was he? He was Nick O'Donovan, a man who lived on the raw edge of life, a legend. And he was her husband's best friend.

The material slipped through her fingers and Catherine closed her eyes. "Why does that make me feel so guilty?"

When she finally opened her eyes again, her vision was blurred by unshed tears. Everyone said the hardest times would be at night, alone. But they were wrong. The happy moments were the hardest and saddest to endure. Whenever something wonderful, or exciting happened, she always wanted to turn and share it, but she couldn't. Most of the time, she remembered and stopped herself, but sometimes she'd—God, how it hurt to actually turn and see that Gideon was really gone. Forever.

She rubbed her arms against a cold that came from within. "I need a new friend, Gideon. I need Nick."

Her palms slapped against the arms of the chaise lounge and she stood. "More than that, I need to be in love again," she whispered to herself. "I want to feel alive again, and Nick makes me feel that way."

But love came with no assurances. She began to pace, remembering how deeply it hurt to lose Gideon. She never wanted to lose anyone again. It hurt too much, she couldn't bear it a second time.

Catherine remained rigid until the salty breeze and the sound of the waves worked their calming effect on her senses. Then she turned and headed into the house.

The clock chimed the hour, but Catherine already knew she'd gone too long without sleep. She also knew it would be light soon, so she stepped to the sliding glass door that faced the beach and began drawing the draperies. Just before a length of white organdy closed off the outside world, Catherine caught a glimpse of a man on the sand below. She quickly opened the curtains again and smiled. It was Nick.

He was still wearing his tuxedo from the night before, but he had rolled the trouser legs up to his knees and was walking in the surf. His jacket and shoes were hooked onto the finger of one hand and slung casually over his shoulder. He was heading toward her pier, but he was staring down as though in deep thought.

She slid the door open and stepped onto the walkway that faced the beach. "Good morning," Catherine called.

Nick looked up and for a second his face was filled with happiness. Then his normal offhand manner returned and he feigned confusion. "Morning?" he questioned, glancing around and appearing too surprised. "Why, so it is."

Catherine watched as Nick stopped directly below her balcony and looked up with a cocky smile. "We've got to stop meeting like this."

She leaned on the railing. "Have you been out here long?"

"I'm not sure. When did we leave Griffith Park last night?"

"Around midnight."

"And what time is it now?"

She glanced at her watch to be sure. "Almost six a.m."

He nodded. "Then I've been out here about six hours."

"Oh, Nick, why didn't you come up?"

He swung the jacket off his shoulder and draped it over his arm. "As a matter of fact, I did, about three times."

Catherine frowned. "I didn't hear you knock."

"I didn't, about three times." His grin was sheepish. "Looks like I wouldn't have woken you up if I had knocked."

She looked down at her evening gown. "No," was all she could answer. Then she remembered his parting words. "I thought we were never going to see each other again?"

"I'm still having trouble with this dialogue stuff. I mean, it was a great line, but I forgot that nothing on this earth could keep me from seeing you again."

"That was sweet, Nick," Catherine said, but then another thought entered her mind. She rested her chin in her hand as she leaned forward on her elbow. "What about Bunny?"

"What about her?"

"The two of you seemed pretty involved last night."

Nick looked up and smiled. "We did?"

"Yes," Catherine snapped.

Nick nodded proudly. "Good."

"Personally, I don't think she's right for you, Nick."

"No, she's not. It was all an act. I'm just glad it worked."

Catherine softened. "You mean you were trying to make me jealous?"

"You? Naw! Sidney. Bunny's been in love with him since the day he hired her as his secretary. I was just helping her out. She thought if Sidney saw her out socially, his interest might pick up."

"I had no idea she liked Sidney. I think that's wonderful."

"Wonderful? It's incredible."

"Are you sure, Nick?"

"Hell, yes, that's the most incredible thing I've ever heard."

Catherine glared at him. "I meant, are you sure that she's got a crush on him?"

"Crush is definitely too mild a word for what she feels for that little man. It's beyond me."

"Well, I think your act worked. Sidney was more than slightly interested in Bunny all evening."

"And what about you?"

"I wasn't interested in Bunny at all."

Nick laughed. "You certainly acted interested."

"Amused is the word I'd use."

"Jealous is the word I'd use." He placed his fists on his red satin cummerbund. "Come clean, weren't you even the tiniest bit envious?"

"I was green."

"Good."

"Oh, Nick. What are we going to do about you and me?"

"I don't know. This strictly friends stuff just isn't going to work."

"You're right, but every time I think of us as anything else... well, I think about Gideon and..."

He shifted his weight and tugged at his unbuttoned collar as though it were still too tight. "You've just got to stop thinking about the past so much."

"I know, but—"

"Catherine, I'm not condemning you for looking back, it's a very natural thing to do, especially here in California. I think everyone on the west coast does it, somewhat."

He rubbed at the stubble that shadowed his chin. "Everything here reminds us of it. There's Sunset Boulevard, Sunset Beach, Sunset restaurants, and a thousand other Sunset whatevers that seem to say that watching the sun go down, and looking back on the past is where all importance lies." His dark eyes pleaded for understanding as he added, "But don't you see, Catherine? They're wrong."

Nick nodded toward the inland sky. "If you want proof, just look."

She followed his gaze and saw rose-colored clouds changing to mauve as fingers of gold began to reach above the craggy walls of the palisades.

"You see, Catherine, the sun also rises. In fact, it always rises."

She stared at the kaleidoscope of colors that transformed the sky into a giant mosaic. There was a long silence, then she said, "You're right, Nick. Yesterday is gone. It's a new day, a new life."

He gave a satisfied nod, then started away.

She blinked in surprise. "You're leaving?"

"Yeah." He paused and turned. "Is there something wrong with that?"

"But what about us?" She ran her forefinger along the rail. "Where do we go from here?"

"I don't know. I hadn't thought that far ahead yet."

"Oh." Her voice was small. "Well, don't you think we should think about it?"

"I think it's best we do nothing right now."

Her voice rose an octave. "What do you mean, nothing?" Catherine looked at him and tried to decide whether to be angry or hurt.

Nick sighed. "Look, neither of us has had any sleep and I think that should be our first priority."

A feeling of déjà vu swept through her as she asked, "But when will I see you again?"

"Who knows." He used his hand to punctuate his next statement. "Catherine, you've got to remember, I'm not the type of guy who likes to be tied into a relationship."

"I know. But you've got to remember something, too. I'm the type of woman who is used to a traditional relationship."

"If you're looking for a commitment—"

"I'm not," she interrupted. "I would just like to have some idea of what to expect and when."

"All right. The next time I'm in the area, I'll drop in and we'll see what happens."

She lifted her eyebrows and said unenthusiastically, "Sort of play it by ear?"

"Right!"

"Right," Catherine repeated flatly.

"You go get some sleep now," Nick said, starting away again.

Catherine nodded, but her mind was still analyzing what had just happened as she turned and started back into the house.

"Oh, yeah," Nick called over his shoulder, "there's one other thing."

She stopped in the doorway. "What?"

"I'll be in the area around noon today."

Catherine smiled with relief. "So, what should one wear when one is playing it by ear?"

He was backing farther away. "Damned if I know, but a swimsuit under slacks and a pair of hiking shoes would probably be nice."

She hurried to the rail. "You know what?"

"What?"

"I like you. I really do."

"I kinda like you too."

* * *

Standing at the bow of a stubby amphibian boat, Catherine wondered if the afternoon really was exceptionally beautiful, or if it was just her mood that made it feel that way. She drummed happily on the safety rail and looked at Nick.

"This is great! I haven't been to Catalina in ages."

Nick smiled. "I'm glad you like the idea." He stared ahead to the rugged mountainous island, which was split by a low isthmus, then he looked back toward the city, which sprawled beyond the flat sandy beaches of Los Angeles. "They say that buccaneers and smugglers used to hide out on Catalina. Maybe we can find one of those secret places and hide from the world, too...."

Catherine's mind was already window-shopping along Crescent Avenue. "I'd love to get lost at this great little boutique I know...."

"Wouldn't it be great to go horseback riding into the interior, and leave civilization behind us...."

"Last time I was there, they had the most adorable lavender dress on display...."

"I know this secluded cove that would be perfect to go snorkeling...."

"It's probably gone by now, but it would have been perfect to wear dancing at the Casino tonight...."

"And tonight we can camp out under the—huh? What did you say?"

"Camp out?" Catherine asked as his words finally soaked into her thoughts.

"Go dancing?" he questioned, just as shocked.

They stared at each other for a moment, then laughed. When their laughter faded, Nick hooked his arm over her shoulders. "Isn't it strange how two people can go to the same place and see it so completely differently from each other?" He gave her a playful squeeze. "If it's shopping and dancing you want, it's shopping and dancing you'll have."

"No," Catherine said, enjoying the feel of his arm around her. "I've done that, dozens of times before. Today I feel like discovering something new. Show me your Catalina."

"It's beautiful," he said dreamily. "Sometimes even breathtaking." He pulled back and looked at her. "But I'm sure it's not as beautiful as you'd be in that lavender dress in the Casino ballroom."

She looked across the water to the huge fortress-like landmark, with its gleaming white walls and red tile roof. The entire top floor was a ballroom that was lush with the romantic atmosphere of the forties. For a moment she pictured the two of them, swaying to the big band sounds. Then the picture shattered—that wasn't Nick's style.

She knew she had to stop trying to shape and mold him to the things she was comfortable with. Looking up into his shimmering brown eyes, Catherine spoke her thoughts aloud. "I don't care what we do as long as we're together."

"Well, I had thought we'd go exploring, but the terrain is pretty rough. The roads, if you can call them that, only go a little way into the interior. Think you're up to it?"

"Obviously, you are not aware that I am the granddaughter of Mary Catherine Benton-Ward, who crossed Europe, sailed an ocean and walked halfway across this continent to join in the Cherokee Land Run, where she staked and held her land despite several attempts by claim jumpers."

Nick laughed. "Was that a yes?"

"Yes. Somewhere in me I'm bound to have some of her grit."

The boat whistle sounded their approach to the dock, and Nick led her toward the exit ramp. "May I assume that the granddaughter of such a courageous woman has been horseback riding before?"

"Yes," Catherine lied. After such a boisterous buildup of her heritage, she hardly felt like admitting the only horse she had ever ridden had been on a merry-go-round.

As they strolled down the Green Pleasure Pier, Nick explained his plans for the day. "Spencer Lord has a ranch here, just outside of Avalon. He's got horses we can ride, and diving equipment if we want to use it. He even has a cabin cruiser we can take out tonight and search for flying fish."

"Sounds like an exciting and full day," Catherine said as he motioned her toward one of the many jitneys that lined the wide boulevard. She climbed in and seated herself only seconds before the driver jerked the bus into gear and they lurched off. Catherine couldn't resist one last look at the beautiful quaint civilized town of Avalon. Then she looked at the mountains that rose at the edge of the town. Horseback riding! Diving! Boating! She hoped she had more of her grandmother in her than she realized, and she hoped she had plenty of liniment in her medicine cabinet.

A few minutes later they stepped off the jitney at a ranch that lay in a deep canyon. From the shadowy archway of an adobe building, an old man came toward them. The stern set of his jaw made him appear to be less than happy to greet them.

Noting that the man looked meaner with each step that brought them closer, Catherine began to doubt Nick. "Are you sure this is Spencer's ranch, and these people know you?"

"Trust me," Nick said with a wink. "Roberto just has to get close enough to see me. His eyes are getting worse."

Suddenly the old man's tan leathery face crinkled into a straight white smile. "Nick! Is that really you?"

Nick beamed. "One and the same."

The man slapped his meaty palm into Nick's hand. Catherine stepped back and watched the two men pump their arms only once before Nick pulled Roberto close, and they happily patted each other's back.

"Nick O'Donovan," Roberto said. "You old picaro."

Nick pulled back. "Look who's calling me an old rascal."

They laughed again and patted each other once more, then Nick faced Catherine. "Roberto is the best horse trainer this side of the Rio Grande."

"*Si,*" the man said, beaming proudly. "I am also best riding instructor. Nick and Gideon, they come to studio to be in Western and they know nothing, *nada*, about horse." He held up two fingers. "In couple hours I teach them everything. Now can ride like Clint Eastwood."

"Nice to meet you, Roberto. I've heard a lot about you."

Roberto looked at Nick. *"Esposa?"*

"Wife?" Nick repeated, taken aback. "Er, no, she's not my wife."

Catherine realized the old man had noticed her wedding ring, and she quickly put her hands behind her back, but not before Nick saw she was wearing it. He sobered, then forced a smile. "I'm sorry, I should have introduced you. Roberto, this is Catherine Har—this is Catherine, a friend."

She exchanged greetings with Roberto, but she was painfully aware of Nick's scrutiny. The old man sensed the awkwardness of the situation and quickly excused himself to get their gear. Nick offered to help and started to follow, but Catherine reached out and stopped him.

"I'm sorry, Nick."

He looked down at the gold band on her hand, which held his arm. "There's nothing to be sorry for. Why shouldn't you wear it?"

"I don't want to keep living in the past, but I can't deny that the past existed either."

He shrugged out of her hold. "Why don't you go pick out a horse while I help Roberto?"

Catherine watched him disappear into the tack room and felt a bittersweet tug at her heart. It had been so hard to finally say that it was time to let go of the past, but now saying it seemed extremely easy compared with actually doing it.

A few minutes later, Nick and Roberto returned carrying the saddles and other things that Catherine didn't recognize. She forgot her inner dilemma as she wondered how to tell Nick that she'd never been around a horse in her life.

"Did the *señora* find a horse to her liking?" Roberto asked, hoisting a saddle onto the top rail of the corral fence.

She threw a quick glance toward the animals. "I'll take the reddish-brown one over there."

"The bay with black points?" Nick questioned, surprised.

Catherine took another quick look at the horses and nodded.

"That one's pretty spirited," Nick offered as Roberto approached the horse, and it began to dance in leery apprehension.

"Yes, I see it has a lot of spirit." She swallowed. "How wonderful." Catherine watched the animal's obvious defiance at the sight of the bridle and bit, and reminded herself there was nothing to be afraid of. After all, she'd seen enough movies to know what should be done.

Nick threw a blanket over the back of a chestnut mare. "This is a fine lady here," he rubbed his hand along its flaxen mane. "She's very gentle."

Casting a quick look at the bay-colored stallion, who was prancing and snorting despite Roberto's soothing words, Catherine moved beside Nick. "Maybe gentle would be a nice change of pace," she said, "just this once."

Nick threw the saddle on the mare's back. "Catherine, have you ridden much?"

"Don't be absurd."

He finished clinching the flank strap and leveled a disbelieving stare at her.

She shrugged. "Does it show that much?"

"I've been a stunt rider for years and I wouldn't pick that stallion." He tucked his bottom lip under and whistled to Roberto. "Forget the bronc. I'll take the black one and she'll use this mare."

Nick placed his hands on her shoulders and positioned her directly in front of the horse. Catherine gave a nervous smile. "Big, aren't they?"

"Pet her," Nick ordered.

Catherine rolled her eyes. "Is this something you feel strongly about?"

"Pet her!"

Cautiously, she reached out toward the animal's face. Nick took her hand and drew it down the broad white mark that extended from the horse's forehead and over the frontal bones.

"This is called a blaze," Nick explained.

The horse nudged its muzzle farther into her hand. Catherine pulled back quickly and ran into Nick's chest. The muscled body she normally admired was now an immovable wall that trapped her too close to a very large animal. Then she felt the rumble of Nick's laughter roll up from his chest.

"She likes you."

"Great," Catherine muttered in disgust.

"Show her that you care, and she'll become very docile."

The horse curled its upper lip and whinnied.

"Listen," Catherine said, "I saw this place in town where we could rent mopeds."

"Forget it," Nick said, again leading her by the shoulders. "Time for your riding lesson."

Her loud protests were ignored as he lifted her into the saddle. She continued with a string of nonstop objections, but Nick turned a deaf ear toward her as he walked her horse until they were next to his. After mounting his gleaming black horse, Nick winked and started leading them around the corral.

The mare had an easiness to her walk and Catherine soon began to relax. Roberto sat on the fence railing and shook his head as he watched Nick take them around in patient circles.

Finally the old man cupped his hand to the side of his mouth. "Give her the reins now, or you'll still be here at midnight."

Catherine's grip on the saddle horn tightened as Nick offered the leather reins to her. "No, thanks."

"Come on," Nick urged. "You'll do fine."

Reluctantly she took her own reins and listened to Nick explain again how to use the thin leather straps to control the huge horse. To her surprise, the mare didn't seem to notice the change in power, and Catherine breathed a sigh of relief.

"See, *señora*, nothing to it," Roberto encouraged as he swung the gate open.

"You mean we're going out there?" she questioned with a nervous laugh.

"You're doing fine," Nick answered.

After a couple of large circles around the stable area, Nick pointed toward a rugged-looking mountain that was to be their destination. Catherine squared her shoulders and urged her horse onward as Nick and Roberto exchanged a few parting words in Spanish.

"What did he say?" Catherine asked, as Nick rode up beside her.

"He was just reminding me that the mare was trained as a stunt horse for the studio."

"So?"

"Don't clap or anything like that, because she'll think it's a movie clapboard and spring into action."

Chapter Eight

Catherine couldn't remember when she had spent a more exhilarating afternoon. When they first left the ranch they followed a trail. It was roughly hewn and in places almost overgrown, but at least it was a trail, a trail that Nick soon abandoned.

As they traversed the canyons and plains, Nick proved himself to be an excellent guide. He explained that because of Catalina's geographic separation from the mainland, there were plants and trees that were indigenous only to the island, and he was quick to point them out to her. Nick also knew the exact spot where a sea lion colony lived below a sheer cliff. Together they watched the noisy young pups playfully lumbering among a group of northern elephant seals that lay perfectly still like huge living rocks.

Afterward they traveled back inland where, among other things, they caught sight of a fawn in a thicket of rare Catalina ironwood. But the most heart-stopping moment came a few minutes later when Nick led her through the middle of two dozen grazing buffalo.

As they moved cautiously among the large woolly animals, Nick explained that the herd, which now numbered over four hundred, had gotten its start from fourteen bison that had been left there when the movie, *Vanishing American*, was filmed on the island in 1924. He kept assuring her that everything would be fine if they didn't make any sudden moves, and between flashes of imagining herself trampled in a stampede, Catherine found the experience thrilling.

By midafternoon, Catherine had begun to feel comfortable with the mare, but she paced her horse quite a bit slower than Nick. She was surprised at how often her eyes were riveted to the rippling muscles on his back, instead of on the mountainous terrain. Nick's rugged features and tall physique were enough to excite any woman, but it was more than just his looks that Catherine found herself attracted to. What fed her continuing desire to be near him, to know him, was the mysterious soul of the man inside the well-defined body.

When the late-afternoon sun began to cast long shadows over the trees and across the mountains, she realized that she had no idea where they were. In her beloved L.A., Catherine was able to navigate the numerous freeways with great ease, but there, among the chaparral and island oak, she had no sense of direction. She was about to ask Nick where they were headed when it came, like an unexpected gift.

They crested a low mountain ridge and there, spread before them like a treasure waiting to be found, was a magnificent shoreline. They were on the windward side of the island, and from the top of the cliff their view was awe inspiring.

"Come on," Nick said, urging his horse down a tiny path carved against the side of the tall cliff.

"You want me to go down that?"

"No, I want you to stay on your horse and let her bring you down. It's pretty sheer, but she'll do all the work if you let her."

Catherine was beginning to feel tired. "Why can't she just work her way back to the ranch?"

Nick stopped, raised himself slightly and turned in the saddle to face her. "Well, we can go back if you want, but there's a low bluff down there that extends out over a very secluded cove. I thought it would be nice to let the horses rest while I show you the most beautiful little beach on this whole island. But if you'd rather not?"

"Well," she said, eagerly, "I think we should let the horses rest awhile."

On the steep descent, Catherine learned why cowboys love their horses. She held her breath most of the way, but the mare's surefootedness delivered her safely to the low bluff just above the beach.

Nick tied off the horses as Catherine let her anticipation rise. It was a lovely place, and she smiled, imagining herself sitting in the tall wheat-colored grass with Nick stretched out beside her, the two of them talking into the twilight. Anxious to bring her plan to life, she swung her left leg over the hind bow of her saddle and started to dismount. Suddenly Nick's hands circled her waist, then he lowered her to the ground.

When he released her, Catherine faced him. He pressed his palms against the horse's neck and loin, his arms like a fortress, surrounding, protecting, and trapping her.

Nick molded his body to hers as he leaned closer. She could feel his hot breath on her already warm skin, and a heady excitement began to build inside her. No longer seeming to have a will of her own,

Catherine lifted her gaze and stared into his luscious brown eyes. She saw the same passion in his eyes as she had seen the night before on the carousel.

His lips parted slightly, and she was sure he was going to kiss her. She closed her eyes, feeling him only a breath away from her own lips. Her whole body tingled as she waited, but instead of a kiss, she heard a curse. She opened her eyes just as his fist slammed into the hard leather of the saddlebag. The surprised mare danced a sidestep, leaving Catherine without anything to lean on. She pitched backward, but Nick caught her wrists and hauled her upright. He pulled her against his length and held her tight. His face was lined with anger, but Catherine wasn't sure at who, or what.

He started to speak, then didn't. Abruptly he released her, spun on his heel and strode across the bluff. Nick stopped at the top of a dirt trail that led to the beach a few yards below. She could tell he was waging a war with himself, wanting to look back, not wanting to; needing to say something, denying that need. Then, with a grim look of determination, he disappeared down the path.

Catherine could feel her pulse pounding at the side of her neck. Each breath she tried to draw seemed to catch in her throat and her thoughts reeled. Their relationship was so crazy. It was all or nothing. They were either awkwardly polite, or mindlessly driven by their desires. She couldn't seem to find the middle of the road. Slowly, as composure worked its way through her mind and body, she followed him to the edge of the bluff.

Nick was busy unfolding a tarp that covered a dinghy that had been beached near an outcropping of rocks. His voice sounded calm and matter of fact when he spoke. "I asked Roberto to have some of the guys from the ranch tow it out here behind the sailboat," he explained.

"What's in it?" Catherine asked, heading down the path. She was relieved that he was acting normally, yet frustrated that there was so much left unspoken.

"Our ticket to a new world," Nick called over his shoulder.

Catherine glanced around, not sure of what he meant. "I kind of like this world," she said, stuffing her hands in the back pockets of her slacks. "Especially today." She paced up and down the small beach of the cove. "You've shown me things I've never seen before, except in books or on television."

He was rummaging through the equipment packed in the small boat, but at her statement he looked up.

Nick's face was full of doubt. "Have you really enjoyed this?"

"Sure," she answered. He made a serious study of her, and she grew embarrassed as his stare continued. Trying to act nonchalant, she bent and picked up a calico scallop shell. "Why wouldn't I enjoy it?" she asked.

He shrugged and started to dig through the equipment again. "I don't know. It's just, well, you know, this isn't a regular date or anything."

"No, it's not," she said, looking up. The disappointment he tried not to show would have broken her heart had she not been ready to add, "It's better than a regular date."

He folded his arms on the rim of the boat and looked at her. "You know, Catherine, you make it very easy to like you." Then spotting something, he delved into the equipment again. "Aha!" he said, triumphantly holding up a compressed air tank.

Catherine blinked. "We're going to go scuba diving now?" she asked, hesitantly.

"Yes. You've been before, haven't you?"

She nodded, moving closer to him. "Down at Portuguese Bend in Abalone Cove, but—"

He waved off her protest. "That's for sissies."

"You keep forgetting something, Nick. Basically I am a sissy."

"Nonsense. I've seen you in the surf before. When you tried to save me, remember?" His eyes glazed as he replayed that morning in his mind's eye. "Lord, but you were a vision coming out of all that horrible white water."

Yes, she remembered the morning.

Nick shook his head as if to free himself from the memory, then he handed her an assortment of scuba gear. "You're a strong swimmer, and you'll do fine here in the kelp beds."

Catherine sighed, feeling more tired than before. She let the equipment slide out of her hands on the wet sand. "Nick, I don't want to go diving or riding again or anything."

The confusion on his face was too ludicrous to be anything but honest. "You don't?"

"No."

"What do you want to do then?"

"Can't we just sit and talk?" she said, simply.

"Talk?"

"Yeah, you've heard of it, haven't you?"

"Sure, but why now, why here?"

Catherine lifted her hands in a hopeless gesture. "Why not?"

He considered her answer a moment, then nodded and folded his arms across his chest as he leaned against the boat. "Anything in particular you want to discuss?"

"Oh, I don't know. We could start with you and me. Us."

"So," he said, unfolding his arms and resuming his search in the boat. "It's going to be that kind of talk."

"Nick, I'd like to just sit and talk for a while. You know, get to know each other like a man and a woman who are attracted to each other normally do."

"But that's so—" he paused trying to think of the right word, then frowned "—it's so—you know."

"Ordinary?"

"Right," he snapped, pointing at her with a fin. "I thought you said you were having a good time even though it wasn't a regular-type date."

"I did, and I am, but I think we've wasted enough time, and I don't mean just today. I'm referring to all the wasted time denying there was anything happening between us. All the guilt. All the empty days of hoping you'd drop by or call or anything. And now, finally, we've gotten past all that, but are we talking? No. Are we holding hands? No. Are we doing anything to advance our relationship? No! All we're doing is creating our own little *Wide World of Sports.*"

"Jim McKay would be proud."

"Nick!"

"Okay," he said, holding his hands up in submission. "I was just trying to add some levity. Geez, woman, you have a temper at times." He gave a low humorless laugh. "You and Gideon must have been a perfect match. He loved to talk, too, and it wasn't just chatter, but deep demanding analyzing talk. Whereas I admired, even envied, that quality in Gideon, I want to remind you, lady, it is not a quality that I possess."

"It's just that communicating feelings is very important to me and I wish it was at least somewhat important to you."

"It is. I've been communicating with you all afternoon."

"I didn't hear anything."

"Then you weren't listening."

Catherine's eyes flashed. "I was too. I was listening and hoping and praying with all my heart that you'd say someth—"

"Catherine! Communication between two people does not always consist of a verbal dialogue."

Her eyes flashed. "It does unless both of you are clairvoyant. Which I'm not."

"Open your mind, for God's sake. Catherine, think a minute. Didn't you learn anything about me today?"

She wanted to say no, but she had learned a lot about him. It was all subtle, but nonetheless, she had picked it up. Damn! She hated it when he was right and she was wrong, so she lied, "I didn't learn anything about you."

"Come on, there are bound to be some things you discovered that you didn't know before."

She thought a moment. "Well, I did learn one thing."

"What?" he asked, anxiously.

"That you can now ride like Clint Eastwood."

"Okay, good. That's a start at least."

"But I learned that from Roberto, not you."

"Well, I'm sorry you didn't learn anything about me, because I learned a lot about you."

"No, you didn't. You couldn't have, we didn't talk. Do you realize that you don't know anything about my life before I met Gideon?"

"Those types of things aren't important to me. I don't care if you were an only child or one of a dozen. It doesn't matter where you grew up, or if you were popular in high school, or who you voted for in the last presidential election. None of those things would make one bit of difference to how I feel about you."

"They might make a difference if you knew them."

"They wouldn't. What did make a difference was that bringing you here today I saw everything new again, through your eyes. It was beautiful. I thought we were sharing something wonderful."

"Well, Nick, you may go for long periods without talking, but when you do decide to say something, it's nice. I don't know what to say."

He nodded toward the pile of gear at her feet. "Put on your gear and say you'll let me show you that new world."

"To be honest with you, I tried it, and diving isn't one of my top ten favorite things to do."

"You probably didn't have a good guide before. I promise to show you things you've never seen."

"You already have. Let's leave it at that."

"Where's your sense of adventure?"

She nodded toward the glowing orange ball on the horizon. "The sun is starting to set."

"All the better. The evening tide will stir up everything down there, and the fish will come out to eat. We'll get to see rush hour in the ocean."

"We'll see nothing, it'll be dark soon."

He produced an underwater lantern and waved it at her.

"What about sharks?" she asked.

"Only if we're lucky."

"Lucky? Hey, Nick, I saw *Jaws*. I don't consider getting maimed or killed, lucky."

"That was celluloid fiction. This is the Pacific. It's Catalina, so if we're lucky all we'll get to see is an angel shark, who'll be more scared by us than we'll be of him."

"Speak for yourself, O'Donovan."

He winked and handed her a wet suit. "Any other questions?"

She sighed. "Where do I change?"

"Right here," he answered, pulling his cable knit sweater over his head. He stopped with it halfway down his arms. "You did wear your swimsuit under your clothes, didn't you?"

Catherine didn't realize she was staring at him until then. She cleared her throat, but her "Yes" was still husky.

"Good," he said, unfastening the snap on his jeans.

Catherine felt embarrassed and confused as she tried not to watch Nick strip down to his swim trunks. He seemed oblivious to her presence, but she couldn't ignore his closeness. An odd sense of timidity and arousal accompanied Catherine as she hesitantly began to unbutton her pink gingham shirt.

She was grateful that she'd worn a maillot instead of a two-piece and hurriedly put on the diving equipment. Just as she was about to complete her task, the zipper on the jacket of her wet suit became stuck halfway up.

Nick handed her a pair of fins and two neoprene foam boots. She pulled them on as fast as possible and began jerking on the zipper again. Nick gave her a curious glance, and she stopped, trying to appear casual. He smiled as though he'd noticed nothing and turned toward the boat to retrieve the insulated gloves and weight belts. Again she tugged on the pull tab, but the slide wouldn't move beyond her bust line.

Nick shrugged into the harness that held his air tank, then held one out for Catherine. She stepped closer to him and turned around. He slipped the straps over her arms and placed the cylinder so that it rested comfortably against her back.

"Aren't you going to ask?" he questioned, flipping the pressure and regulator hoses over her shoulder.

She faced him. "Ask what?"

"For some help with that."

"I can do it myself," she said, then saw his hands moving toward the front of her jacket.

He brushed her hands to the side as his large ones took hold of the zipper. Her breathing quickened, but again he appeared not to notice as he continued talking calmly. "I said you were easy to like, but did I mention you're a little too independent?"

With one quick tug, the pull tab slid up, closing her heaving breasts behind the tight fitting material. "Thank you," she mumbled, turning away. "Now, can we get on with this expedition?"

"Your barge awaits, mighty queen," Nick said, indicating for her to hop in as he shoved the dinghy into the surf.

Nick maneuvered the boat around the craggy rocks that jutted up from the ocean floor. Then he cut the motor and dropped the anchor as soon as they cleared the last rock. He sat on the edge of the boat checking his gear. "Would you believe that down there is a world that rivals L.A. in sheer abundance of life?"

"But are the natives friendly?" she asked, pretending to check her own gear.

He laughed. "Ready?"

Catherine looked at the surface of the water, which was almost entirely covered with giant plumes of kelp. With a sigh, she inserted her mouthpiece and nodded. Nick leaned back and dropped into the gray-green water. Catherine closed her eyes and followed him.

She felt herself hit the ocean with a splash, then she began to float downward. Something brushed her hand and Catherine gasped, sucking in too much air. Her lungs burned and her eyes watered, but what hurt worse was her feeling of foolishness when she realized it had only been Nick.

He took her hand in his, and they looked at each other in a long silent stare. Everything else faded from her thoughts. She didn't notice the hideous mask or the regulator hose; all she saw were Nick's dark eyes smiling at her. When he looked at her that way, he didn't need to talk, he said it all through his eyes.

She reminded herself how very wrong it would be for both of them if she judged his actions according to what she'd known with Gideon. Nick O'Donovan was his own man, and it was that man that she was attracted to. She had to accept the fact that Nick would never be as open about his feelings as Gideon had been. Nick's inner thoughts were his, and if he shared them with her, it would be rarely.

Nick motioned for her to look up, and when she did she saw that the tall fronds reaching for the surface had formed a swirling canopy above them. The setting sun was slanting its long rays into the water, creating sparkling shafts of light that penetrated the underwater forest.

Nick squeezed her hand, then pointed down with his other hand, and they began to swim through the blue-green tropical jungle that grew from the submerged cliffs. Nick led them against the tidc that swayed the giant kelp. Catherine wasn't sure she could have fought the rushing water without his help. She was so busy concentrating on her lack of strength that they were well into the middle of a school of blacksmiths before she realized it. The determined-looking fish seemed unconcerned by the foreign presence among them as they continued searching for the food that was carried in the current.

As they dove deeper toward the sloping seafloor, Catherine began to enjoy their weightless world that was becoming darker and darker. Following the small beam from Nick's underwater light, they encountered a garibaldi, whose silver-rimmed eyes studied them as they, in turn, studied the brilliant orange color of its graceful body. Then a silvery squid glided past them, glistening more than usual against the backdrop of dark ocean water.

Catherine felt a sense of renewal and was ready to explore the black infinity forever, but Nick finally stopped and pulled her up short. She maneuvered herself around to face him. He turned the beam of light onto his wristwatch and Catherine couldn't believe how quickly the time had passed. Reluctantly she nodded that they should head toward the surface, but as they turned back something flashed before her eyes.

She stopped and looked around in every direction. Nick turned to face her and shrugged to question what was wrong. Catherine placed her hand over the light, then Nick saw what she had seen. He quickly turned off the lantern, allowing them to hover in a world of black and silver. Everything, including Nick and Catherine, was covered with minute specks that glowed like stars in a faraway galaxy. The movement of their feet and arms created thousands of tiny explosions of glittering light. Finally Nick pulled her on, but Catherine couldn't keep from looking back at their sparkling iridescent wake.

A half hour later Catherine sat on the deck of a cabin cruiser that had been waiting for them when they surfaced. Roberto had earlier taken two other men to shore to ride the horses back to the ranch, and now the old man was tossing a salad while Nick grilled the steaks.

"Honestly," Catherine said to an attentive Roberto, "it was the most incredible thing I've ever seen.

Like thousands and thousands of glittering little stars."

"Bioluminescence," Nick explained, adding more seasoning to the sizzling meat.

"Biolumi—what?" Roberto asked.

"The common name is sea fire," Nick said.

"Oh, *si*. Sea fire. Is most beautiful. Very evident around Santa Catalina."

"Well, whatever it was, I'll never forget it." Catherine stood and indicated their hard work. "Are you two sure that there's nothing I can do? Surely I can—"

"Nothing," Nick said. "Relax."

"Nada," Roberto chimed in. "Like Nick said, is our treat."

"I just feel I should be doing something."

Nick shrugged. "I guess you could dress for dinner if you'd like."

Catherine looked down at her pants and shirt, which she'd pulled on over her bathing suit. "There's nothing I'd like better, but I'm afraid this is all I brought with me."

"I think there are some things in the closet below, if you'd like to take a look." Nick elbowed Roberto in the ribs. "Right, Roberto?"

"Huh? Oh, *si*, *si*. Señor Lord always keep a few negli—er—" he moved his fingers over his chest to indicate something frilly "—you know, uh...things! He always keep a few things on board."

She gave Nick a wary look. "I doubt that one of those things would be appropriate for dinner."

"You never know until you check," Nick said, smiling.

"Okay, I'll go look." She started toward the cabin, but stopped on the top step of the companionway. "You know, I still can't imagine Spencer owning all this. A ranch, horses, a boat, all that scuba gear."

"Señor Lord, he is very rich."

Nick smiled. "I think Catherine knows that, Roberto. What she's trying to figure out is why someone who hardly leaves the studio long enough to eat would have all these things."

Catherine nodded. "Right. I mean, he's so married to his work that he lives in a trailer on the back lot. When does he ever take time to use all this?"

"Is not for him, *señora*."

"Then who's it for?"

"Us," Nick said, waving a large fork between himself and Roberto.

"You two?"

"Not just us, but all the stuntmen."

"I explain," Roberto said. "See, Señor Lord, all his movies they are...oh, what's he call them?"

"Action-packed. High adventure," Nick offered.

"*Si*, and he needs lots of stuntmen always available, but many like Nick, they like to always be active. So to keep them close during filming, or if he might need soon, he bought the ranch for them to use."

"Or," Nick said, "if someone gets hurt they can recuperate here and use the facilities to get back in shape."

"Or if they get too old to do the gags," Roberto said, sadly. "Señor Lord very generous man to give me job as foreman."

Catherine leaned against the companionway. "I'm sure he feels he could never repay your generosity in teaching all those actors and stuntmen how to ride. Not to mention all those years that you trained the horses."

Roberto's chest swelled. "I like her," he said to Nick.

Nick shrugged. "Yeah, she's okay, but she's going to miss dinner if she doesn't hurry. The steaks are almost ready."

Catherine bounced past the galley and the salon. She felt good all the way through. Inside the forward stateroom she stopped in her tracks. A large box was lying on the bunk. Moving closer, she saw that the box was from her favorite boutique on the island, and there was a card attached.

This isn't the Casino ballroom, but I'd still like the first dance tonight. Hope the dress fits.

Nick

Catherine picked up the card and hugged it to her breast. How romantic, she thought, just like something Gideon would have done. Gideon. The name echoed through her mind and she soberly looked down at her wedding ring. A tiny little ache cried out inside her, but she bit her lip and removed the ring. Then, walking to a hanging locker near the door, she opened it. Carefully, and with misty eyes, she placed the single gold band in the large empty locker and quietly closed the door.

Chapter Nine

The steaks were delicious and the dinner conversation delightful. Then Roberto conveniently became tired and took the launch back to the island's marina. Nick found a Willie Nelson tape, plugged the cassette player into the audio system and long past midnight they danced in the moonlight, creating their own "Stardust Memories."

Between songs, they would continue dancing, moving to the beat of the waves against the side of the boat.

"I like the sound of the water against the teakwood," Catherine said without opening her eyes.

"It's very romantic with the two of us here, like this."

"Very," Nick murmured.

"But it must have sounded rather sad when you were alone."

"Most everything is rather sad when you're alone."

"Sidney said you like being alone."

"He's right."

"I didn't think anyone liked being alone. You accept it, you make the best of it, but like? How? Why?"

"It always seemed better than the alternative."

"Being with someone."

"No. Being hurt."

She stopped, lifted her head and looked at him. "Nick, caring about someone doesn't always lead to pain."

Still holding her hand in his, he drew their arms inward and touched the tip of her nose with his finger. "You can relax, darlin', I've decided you're worth the pain." His left hand moved from her waist and gently cradled her head, pressing her into the crook of his shoulder.

Catherine tilted her head back. "I won't hurt you, Nick."

"You already have."

"How?"

"I'll never like being alone as much as I did before. You've ruined it for me."

"I can't say I'm really sorry."

He hesitated for just a beat and looked down at her. "The funny thing is, I'm not sorry either."

The night air on the ocean made the sleek deck of the boat an invitingly cool dance floor for their bare feet, and they swayed without speaking for a long while. Catherine found that as long as she could hold Nick close, she didn't mind the silence.

A breeze fluttered the skirt of her dress. The coolness that snaked up her body reminded her that she wore nothing beneath the dress except a pair of new panties she had found among the things Spencer provided so generously for his numerous guests.

Nick played with her ruffled collar. "We can take the dress back tomorrow," he said.

Catherine waltzed back a step to look down at the baggy dress that she had managed to tuck and sash enough to stay on. "I love it and I love the thought of Roberto trying to explain what size I am to the saleswoman. I don't believe I've ever been described as thin as a filly before."

Nick pulled her back into his embrace. "Don't I get any of the credit? It was my idea."

She breathed in the heady aroma of his cologne. "I love you, too, but that's nothing new."

"Love may not be anything new to you, lady, but it sure is to me. I've never been in love before."

She wanted to look up at him, but she was afraid to. "Are you saying you are now?"

"Well, I'm in something with you. I was hoping you could tell me if it was love or not."

She stopped dancing and ran her fingers up and down the lapels of the corduroy jacket he wore over his sweater. "I'm not a very impartial person to ask, Mr. O'Donovan. You see, I have a vested interest in the outcome of this venture."

"You sound like Sidney," Nick said, shaking his head.

Catherine tossed her head back and laughed, and when she opened her eyes Nick was looking at her as he had never done before. He took in her mouth, her eyes, her hair, and he seemed unable to absorb enough of it. His wandering gaze finally stopped at her eyes, and he captured her soul with his hypnotic stare. He held her gaze in a spellbinding moment of anticipation as he slowly brought his lips closer and closer to hers.

It was a gentle kiss. A warm and tender exploration, a testing of the waters. He was such a contradiction. Most of him appeared rough, but parts of him were velvety soft, like his lips, and his soul, which he tried so hard to hide.

He pulled away and Catherine's heart stopped, until he lifted his mouth slightly and placed a gentle kiss on her temple. Her eyes fluttered shut at his touch. Then he kissed her eyelids, her cheek. Then his lips brushed across hers again, and her breath caught at the brief electric encounter.

Nick moaned and returned to taste her lips fully, completely. Catherine savored the exquisite joy of the moment, only to have him drag his mouth away again. Her disappointment was temporary as he sought and found the softness of her neck. Tiny little kisses were planted in a single row up the side of her neck to her ear. Her senses leapt with such delight that her body trembled.

Nick's hands began to travel up the silky dress. His fingertips teased the tips of her breasts until the peaks strained for more. Then as his tongue flicked at the sensitive core of her ear, a small cry escaped her lips and Catherine arched into him.

Nick groaned and brought his mouth back to brand her with the searing heat of his lips. Her own lips parted, beckoning his tongue, though she knew he needed no invitation. His kiss was a ragged exploration that insisted she join with him, and she did, eagerly.

But his need was too strong, and his desire to have all of her threatened to overpower them both. Nick drew her higher and higher with his demands until she stood up on her toes to try to give him enough. Still he kept taking more and more, until she couldn't breathe.

"Nick," she gasped, nearly collapsing in his arms.

"Oh, God, Catherine," he said, burying his face in auburn strands of her hair.

This was what she had wanted since she first saw Nick on the beach, but a love that was based on a physical attraction frightened her. With Gideon it had been a slow friendly persuasion. Their passion had grown out of their love. A hollow feeling began to gnaw at the warmth inside her, as Catherine wondered if it could work the other way around.

Nick kissed through her hair until he reached her shoulder. "I want you," he mumbled, nibbling at the exposed flesh, but Catherine pulled back slightly.

"Don't, Nick, I can't think when you do that."

His hand slid around her neck, and his thumb moved in a slow circle beneath her chin, then he tilted her face up until she was again staring into his seductive gaze. "I don't want you to think."

"But I have to," she said, breathlessly.

"No, you don't."

"I don't?" she asked, feeling drugged by her own passion.

"The only thing you have to do is make love to me."

Panic rose inside her, but it only made her breath come harder, and her breasts strain more against his chest.

"Now," he said with an urgency that scared her.

"But I'm not . . . ready yet."

Still his thumb massaged her chin, and he kept her gaze locked into his. "Did I tell you how alluring you looked today when we were diving?"

She managed to take a full breath, and the sea air cleared her mind slightly. "In that getup I looked about as sexy as a piece of seaweed." She placed her hands against his chest and shoved. Catherine's strength was no match for Nick's, and she couldn't have moved him if she hadn't caught him off guard.

She started away, but Nick recovered quickly and grabbed her wrist. He pulled her back into his arms and held her tighter than ever. "Lady, I'd like to get tangled in your fronds any day."

"Oh, Nick, don't. I need time to think. I suddenly feel so confused."

"What is there to be confused about? I'm a man, you're a woman. We've just admitted we're in love with each other. Next step?" He tried to kiss her again, but she turned her head, and he only tasted hair. Nick growled wildly and playfully nipped on her earlobe.

"I thought I was ready," she said, fighting to avoid his roving mouth. "But I keep having these doubts. Maybe it's not real."

Nick squeezed her close. "It's real."

"Maybe Sidney's right."

He kissed her cheekbone. "Sidney's never right."

"Maybe you did just come along at a very vulnerable time in my life and . . ."

"All this logic is dangerous."

"I'm not so sure."

He stopped and pulled back, facing her. Then he cupped her face in his hands and stared at her. "Forget Sidney. Forget logic. Tell me what you feel inside, Catherine."

"That I love you," she said, amazed at her own honesty. "And that I can't bear another minute without you."

"Then why are we standing here talking?"

"Because I want to be sure."

"But isn't that the only real certainty in life, that nothing is certain?"

"I just want to be sure that I'm doing this for you and me. I don't want to wake up and find that I was just lonely, or somehow trying to recapture something."

Nick released her and stepped back. "I thought you sorted all this out already?" he asked, his jaw tightening.

"I thought I did, too, but now I'm not so sure."

"So what do we do now?"

"I just need a little more time."

"Oh, yeah," he said in a voice edged with anger. "What about all that wasted time you were talking about today?"

"I was talking about us getting to know each other better."

"I can't think of a better way."

"But that's only one side of us. I'm talking about the side of us that will be there when our passion dies."

"So far it hasn't lived much."

"Believe me, Nick. I want you as much as you want me, but—"

"There's always a but, isn't there?"

"Please, try to understand, Nick. It's just that I want to wake up and find that we've found something new, something that's ours alone."

He finally nodded. "Okay, you win. I'll give you a little more time." He turned, shaking a finger in her face. "But not much."

Catherine tried to laugh, though she felt anything but jovial.

Nick offered her his arm. "May I escort you to your cabin?"

Catherine hesitantly took his arm.

"Relax. I won't push you. A good-night kiss—correction, a good-night peck, that's all."

The walk across the deck seemed unbearably long in the heavy silence that hung between them. At the companionway steps, she forced a lightness into her words. "Well, we never did get to see those famous flying fish you were telling me about."

"Maybe another night," he said, reaching the door to her cabin.

Catherine grabbed the handle and started to open the door, but then she turned and faced him. He was looming over her with one arm leaning on the jamb. Nick easily filled the tiny space with his large body. "Nick, I—"

"Shhh," he said, touching her lips with his finger. "There's no need to say anything. I understand. Take all the time you need."

"Thank you," she said, standing on her toes, and gently kissing the half-moon scar on his cheek.

Nick grabbed her waist with his free arm and pulled her closer. The feel of his lean strong body caused Catherine to shiver, a shiver that deepened in intensity when Nick bent to kiss her. She fought not to let it happen, but her senses betrayed her, and she started to respond as fervently as Nick. Desire rose within her like a phoenix, and she felt dizzy with her need for him.

But with that desire came memories from the past, questions from the future and doubts from only a moment before. She pulled away. "I thought you said I could take all the time I need?" Catherine asked, in a voice husky with her ragged breathing.

"This is all the time you need."

She shook her head, but he was already drawing toward her again. Remembering the handle that she still grasped behind her back, she turned the knob and almost fell back into the cabin as the door opened. "No, Nick. Not yet. I'm not ready."

"I'll be here when you are," he said as she slowly closed him out. She leaned against the door and wished she could close out her emotions as easily. Everything inside her was tumbling, and her knees felt so weak she could hardly stand. She needed to think. She needed to be sure. But Nick was right, she thought, there's nothing in this world we can be certain of. No, she corrected herself, there *is* one thing I'm sure of. To hell with logic and thought.

Grabbing the handle, she swung the door open. "Wait!" she called, then she collided with Nick's tall frame, which still filled the doorway. He hadn't moved an inch, but upon seeing her anxious look, he started forward. Catherine had to back up quickly just to stay ahead of him.

Nick grabbed his jacket from his shoulder and slung it across the room toward the far bunk. Then he kicked the door, slamming it shut. Though his movements were rough and harsh, the look in his eyes was tender, and it drew Catherine toward him.

"Is this all the time you need?" he asked in a thick raspy voice.

She nodded, not saying a word.

Nick pulled his sweater off over his head and stopped with it just below his elbows. "You're sure?"

Afraid to chance her voice, she nodded again.

He tore at the bulky sweater and tossed it somewhere beyond Catherine. His hands went to the snap on his jeans, and again he stopped as if he were afraid to go on. Catherine moved to him, placed her hands over his and pulled the snap open. She took control, and his hands fell away as she slowly released the zipper, bit by bit.

"Damn you're slow," Nick said with a laugh that tumbled from deep inside him.

"But I'm good," she teased, slipping her hands beneath the waistband of his swimsuit.

Nick placed his hands on top of hers, and together they removed his jeans and swim trunks. He stood up, pulling Catherine back up with him, then he stepped back, kicking the clothes out of his way. So sensually aware of his perfect athlete's body was Catherine that she hardly noticed that Nick had grabbed her sash until he tugged on the loose bow. The loops gave easily, and the sash dropped from the waist of the too-large dress, which she wore sarong-style. Folds of lavender silk fell open like a gracefully parting curtain. His dark eyes scanned the smooth curves of her body, then he looked up and smiled.

Feeling an irresistible pull, they drew together in an embrace. He held her tight as though she were a lifeline without which he could not exist. Her breasts were crushed against his hard chest, and she came alive with the throbbing desire of their embrace. They were bound to each other, not just by their passion, but by the overwhelming need to which their passion drove them.

His hands began to roam across her slender back, then up her rib cage. Catherine's breasts rose and fell in exaggerated movements as her breath quickened. Nick's palm cupped the swell of her breast, and as he began a slow circular motion with his hand, their bodies fell into the same rhythm.

Still tantalizing one breast with his hand, he bent and took the other with a kiss. His tongue caressed and sipped her nipple into a blazing peak. She filled her hands with the softness of his thick hair and arched into the hard muscled lines of his body. With a moan that spoke of his undeniable desire, he suddenly pushed her back and scooped her up into his arms.

She enjoyed the ripple of tense muscles beneath her fingers as he lowered her onto the bunk. Nick followed her down, and his body covered hers with a possession that thrilled her quivering body. White-hot flames ignited inside her as she felt the hard throb of his need against her thighs.

Her breath caught as he entered her, and they began the fiery search for a shared ecstasy. Catherine was floating in a sea of passion, drowning in sheer abandonment. Wave upon wave of new desires were washing over her until she could hardly bear it. Suddenly, she clung to him as together they plunged into the infinite depths of their love.

Outside the moonlit porthole a pair of long sleek fish flew out of the water and spread their pectoral fins like wings as they soared high over the bow of the boat. Then they returned to the sea together.

It took several weeks for the afterglow of their time on Catalina to begin to fade, but finally one morning it did. Nick had done everything in his power to keep it from happening, mostly by never giving her a moment alone, but even the carefree Nick O'Donovan had obligations. He had an early-morning meeting one day, and so they spent the night apart. Catherine had expected the loneliness, but it surprised her when Nick called to say good-night because he was feeling lonely.

The next day, as Catherine took her morning walk, she began to realize that they were back in the real world. Rational thoughts bombarded her from every direction. As she watched the hypnotic swells of the ocean, the morning tide began to pull at her thoughts. How strange it was that the sea had gone unchanged for centuries, and yet at the same time, it changed with every passing moment. That was how she felt at the moment, as though nothing had changed, and yet everything had changed.

Slipping her hands into the front pockets of her jeans, Catherine thought of the love she had found with Gideon, and then how she had lost it in what seemed like the same breath. Now Nick was offering her love again, but with a similar chance for sorrow.

Funny, but she had been one of the millions of people who loved to watch the marvelous things that stuntmen did. Then she fell in love with one of them. In a single heartbeat she had gone from admiring the chances they took, to detesting them for risking something as precious as life itself.

Catherine tossed her head back and glanced up the beach toward the pier. The lights on the promenade were reflected in the water like jewels on a mirrored sea. Then, in sets of ten, the lights flickered off. The morning was taking on the blue-gray cast Catherine had always thought was a calculated bleakness so the sunrise could be displayed with more glory.

As the glowing orange sun crested the mountain tops, Catherine shielded her eyes with her hand. "The sun always rises," she said, remembering what Nick had said a few days earlier. "But you forgot to mention that it always sets too."

With Gideon, she had stolen a shining moment between a sunrise and a sunset, and she couldn't help but wonder if she dared to defy the fates and try for happiness again. What if it happened twice? Was that brief taste of joy worth all the possible sorrow? Catherine shook her head. She just couldn't decide.

As she slowly walked toward the pier, she tried to free her mind of everything except the beauty of the shoreline. Bits of abalone shells tickled her feet as a wave splashed over them. Then thousands of the tiny pieces turned their mother of pearl side to the morning sun and shimmered as they washed onto the wet sand.

A small tern scurried along the ebb line, trying to avoid the cold waves as they washed high on the slope of the beach. Catherine stopped to watch the bird's antics, and heard someone trying to sneak up behind her. It had to be Nick.

"O'Donovan, what are you doing back here?" she asked, trying not to let him see how happy she was to see him. "I thought you had an appointment this morning?"

"I canceled it."

"Why?"

"Because I was afraid if I left you alone very long you'd start doing something dangerous."

"Dangerous? No way. You're the only one I know who likes to live that way."

He nodded. "I was right. You've been thinking, and that's really dangerous."

"Yes, I was thinking. I was thinking that life is too precious for people to go around taking unnecessary chances. Gideon had no choice; you do."

He moved closer to her. "Catherine, it wasn't Gideon who took the unnecessary chance, but you. You gambled on the fact that he was cured, and that you'd have years of happiness together, and you lost. That's still no reason to deny us a chance."

"But what if I take a chance again, and something happens to you too?"

"But what if nothing happens, and we miss our chance at happily ever after?"

"Oh, Nick," she said, leaning against him, wishing that she had his strength, his faith.

Suddenly, he spun her sharply around and pointed. "Look!"

It took her a second to focus, then she saw a gull that seemed to be fighting an invisible force above the waves. "What is he doing?"

"Shhh," Nick whispered, his breath feathering through her hair near her ear. "He's trying to catch an air cushion and ride it up. I swear, it'll take him so high that it'll look like he's stepping from cloud to cloud."

Just then the stout little bird caught the thermal. He spread his wings and remained perfectly still for a moment as the air current held him suspended between the earth and the heavens.

"There's only one thing more beautiful," Nick said, "and that's to catch one of those yourself."

She watched the sea gull arch its silvery wings in triumph as it gracefully began ascending in an endless succession of spirals. Catherine smiled. "I've heard that you can follow a bird up, just like that. Is it true?"

"Yes."

She leaned her head back and watched the gull until it was hardly more than a pinpoint in the sky. Then Nick grabbed her hand and pulled her after him.

"Where are we going?"

"I'm going to take you up in a glider. We're going to soar higher than you've ever imagined possible. Who knows, we may go on chasing clouds forever."

Chapter Ten

The whole Los Angeles area appeared to still be sleeping as the Woodie quietly purred along the Pacific Coast Highway. Catherine knew they were heading south, but that was all she really knew about where they were going. Their destination didn't really matter—anywhere was special when she was with Nick.

She rested her head against Nick's shoulder and cuddled near him as she watched the suburbs rolling by. They followed Palos Verdes Drive, which hugged the rugged clifftops, as it wound past palatial homes and fields of wildflowers. The road curved at Point

Fermin Light House and Los Angeles Harbor came into view.

The huge maze of channels, inlets, and islands was host to one of the most diverse ports in the western world. They drove past berths that held gigantic ships in dry dock, while the sparks of welders' tools burned night and day. Cavernous warehouses held everything from seafood canneries to Howard Hughes's infamous *Spruce Goose*. There was even a quaint colonial area on one wharf. It recreated the feeling of a nineteenth-century seacoast village, and next door to it was a simulated Mediterranean seaport complete with bougainvillea and an outdoor bazaar that was lush with semitropical fruits and flowers.

Over the Vincent Thomas Bridge was Terminal Island and the Naval Base. Catherine smiled, ruefully. "Ah, Long Beach and its own unique perfume."

Nick followed her gaze toward several oil derricks. Sitting in shiny black pools, the stripper wells never ceased their endless pumping from the salty bogs, while in a nearby channel, a small fleet of tuna clippers made their way to the sea. "It's an odd mixture all right, salt water and fish and oil."

"It always reminds me of men who work with their hands. Like my grandfather, he was an oil man, a real wildcatter. He was there when the Mary Sudik blew."

"The who blew?"

"The Mary Sudik in Oklahoma City."

"Strange name for an oil well."

"It was the name of the woman who owned the farm they were drilling on. When she blew they couldn't stop her for eleven days. It was incredible."

"I always wanted a grandfather to tell me stories about other places, other things."

"You didn't have one?"

"Nope, so I just made up my own stories and swore someday I'd make them come true, so I'd have something to tell my grandkids about."

"Providing you live long enough to tell them."

"Don't start on that, Catherine, you'll ruin a perfect day."

She fell silent. Talking about it wasn't going to change anything, and it would ruin the day. As she did so often, Catherine put the thought out of her mind. Though she knew it was illogical, she kept hoping if she didn't let herself think about it, the problem would go away.

Soon the beautiful resort of Newport was presenting its sandy beaches and yacht-filled harbors. When the artist colony of Laguna Beach came and went in a flourish of eucalyptus trees and palms, Catherine couldn't contain herself any longer.

"Where on earth are we going, Nick?"

He smiled. "I told you, soaring."

"Where, Tijuana?"

"Torrey Pines."

"So where's that?"

"Just sit back and relax. We'll be there soon."

A few minutes later they were cruising the main boulevard in La Jolla. The charming little town was just beginning to wake up, even the fog was lingering longer on the ground than usual. Through the mist, which glistened in the morning light, the town sparkled like a golden jewel.

"Oh, Nick, I've always wanted to come down here and check out their shopping. I've heard it's fantastic. They have gobs and gobs of boutiques and specialty shops and art gal—" Seeing the look on Nick's face, her enthusiasm waned. "But then, once you've seen one art gallery, you've seen them all. I mean, they're a dime a dozen up and down the coast. I'd much rather go soaring."

Nick laughed. "No you wouldn't. You'd much rather be turned loose with your gold card in those stores."

She reached up and took his hand, which was resting on her shoulder. "No, Nick. I really wouldn't. I'll admit, I have an occasional relapse, like just now, but honestly, I'd rather be with you. I wouldn't have believed it a few months ago, but I'm actually growing fond of all the things we do together outdoors."

"Even if it's a lie, I love you for it."

"It's not a lie. I'm beginning to understand why you hate the confines of a normal life. We have such freedom when we're skiing or sailing or soaring, I suppose."

"And don't you get a certain thrill while you're doing these things?"

She faced him. "Yes, but not the type of thrill you seek with your stunts."

"Aw, come on, it's almost the same."

"No, Mister O'Donovan, it's not. When we're flying, we're inside the plane, not hanging on the wing by our fingernails. And when we four-wheeled across Baja, you were under the steering wheel, not being dragged beneath the wheels by a rope. And when we dine on the top floor of a building, we leave by the elevator, not by dropping into an air bag three hundred feet below."

"You forgot, O'Donovan roasting as an open fire," he sang with sarcasm.

"I was just getting around to that."

"Well, forget it, we're here."

They had taken a road that joined with the old coast highway on a mesa. Eucalyptus trees were as commonplace in Southern California as palm trees, but there, on the plateau, they grew in thick, mighty forests. But what took her breath away were the groves of pine. They were twisted, with wind-shaped trunks and with branches and roots so gnarled it was hard to tell which was which.

"They're like sentinels at the shore," Catherine said, hardly aware she was talking aloud.

"Yes," Nick said, "they must have looked much the same when Cabrillo first saw them clinging to these cliffs hundreds of years ago."

"I would have loved California then."

"Don't you now?"

"Sure, but imagine how it must have looked when it was almost untouched."

Nick stopped the car suddenly and faced her. "There are still places out there that are almost untouched. We could find them together."

"Oh, Nick, I'm not an adventurer like that. I love to imagine other times, but it's all fantasy. I'm not the type to up and sail away on uncharted seas. Someone else will have to discover the new places, and I'll read about it in my *National Geographic*."

"I can show you places that you can't even imagine."

She stared into his dark brown eyes. "Nick, do you still feel the need to escape?"

"Sometimes."

Catherine hadn't thought the words would hurt her so deeply. "Is it me? Do I made you feel trapped?"

"No. I thought you would. I thought you would smother me, but I was wrong. When I'm with you I feel more free than ever before."

"Then why this need to escape?"

"Not from you, with you. I want to take you off to someplace where the world won't interfere. Somewhere..."

"Over the rainbow?"

"Why not?" Nick said, pounding the steering wheel and leaning back against the bench seat. "Gideon believed in Oz, why can't we?"

"Gideon believed that Oz existed inside us, as does our courage and our brains and our heart."

He pulled himself out of his dreams and pointed to a surrealistic-looking city of concrete that rose above a tall stand of trees. "Come on, Dorothy," he said, shifting into gear. "The Emerald City awaits."

As they drove through the Salk Institute, Catherine did feel somewhat as if she were seeing the Emerald City. The Institute was a four-story structure with wings of concrete, teakwood, and glass, flanking an open court that overlooked the Pacific. She had hardly closed her mouth from viewing the powerful design of the buildings, when they were suddenly facing the sailplane area.

Catherine knew in a moment that Nick was right, she was going to love soaring. They stepped out of the Woodie, and as though they were one, they moved across the mesa toward the launching site. Anticipation gathered in her stomach like clouds before a storm.

She watched as the nose of a sailplane was attached to a cable that was connected to a winch, which extended the length of a runway. A man stood at the tip of the wing, balancing the small plane on its single landing wheel. Then a flagman signaled the winch operator, and Nick grabbed Catherine to keep her from moving closer.

He stood behind her, his arms enclosing her in the warmth of his embrace, and they watched the plane as it was projected, slingshot fashion, off the cliff. The cable was released quickly, and the motorless craft dropped for a second. Catherine's breath caught in her throat, and she flattened herself against Nick for support, but then the wind caught the plane and lifted it up, toward the clouds.

Nick gave her a playful squeeze as the glider soared over the ocean. "Still want to go up?"

She turned in his arms. "More than ever."

Within half an hour Catherine was climbing into the front seat of a sailplane. As Nick strapped her in, she ran her hand over the graceful lines of the sides. His hand covered hers for a moment, and they looked into each other's eyes. He seemed to be trying to say something that he had no words for.

"I love you," she said, without thinking why.

He gave her a pleased, but surprised look. Then a thought came to him, it was clear in his eyes, but he said nothing and started to climb into the pilot's seat.

"Nick, what were you thinking?"

"I just realized that you trust me completely with your life, but you don't trust me with my own life."

She was going to respond, but the wing attendant interrupted. "Mr. O'Donovan, sir, the wind is just right. We need to get you airborne."

"Right," he said, seating himself and closing the canopy.

Catherine had her eyes trained on the edge of the cliff, but from the corner of her eye she saw a flash of color, and she knew the flagman had given the signal. The man dropped the wing tip and pulled back quickly, and at the same moment they were whisked down the runway and shot into the air. There was no moment of hesitation, the wind cupped them immediately and lifted the plane. Catherine clutched her stomach at the sudden sensation and she heard Nick's soft laugh.

She felt as if her soul had been set free. It was almost like a religious experience seeing the world spread below, so close and yet so far. She had flown before, but in regular planes there was so much noise and man-made power. This was different. Nothing separated her from the world but the wind.

"Hold on," Nick said, "I'm going to bank."

His turn was shallow, but it allowed them to be caught in another current that lifted them sharply, then dropped them gently into the low clouds just above the shore.

Catherine looked down through the wisps of cottony white, then she gasped in sudden realization. "Listen," she whispered.

"What?" Nick asked, leaning forward. "I don't hear anything."

"That's it. There's no sound. My God, Nick, this is beautiful. I don't want it to ever end."

And they did keep chasing clouds, though not always in a glider. Nick's whirlwind pace and his constant need for activity didn't give her a chance to consider whether they had been together for hours or days or weeks. All she did know was that she was happy, very happy.

As they strolled down the Walk of the Angels, she realized that she didn't even know what day it was. Catherine knew she should feel guilty for spending so much time away from the restaurant, but it was hard to feel guilt on such a beautiful evening.

There was a balmy breeze blowing that made the night feel as if it were on loan from a tropical isle. Adding to the weather were the marvelous sounds and sights of Olvera Street. Catherine would have sworn they were thousands of miles and hundreds of years away from the large sprawling city of Los Angeles. Instead, they were right in its heart, at the Old Plaza.

They had taken the walking tour starting at the circular, wrought-iron bandstand. On that spot a Spanish governor was said to have founded the pueblo, *El Pueblo de Nuestra Señora la Reina de Los Angeles*. The English translation was, The Town of Our Lady the Queen of the Angels. Later it was shortened to Los Angeles and finally to just, L.A.

Moving around the square, they took in the Old Plaza Church, then headed down the block-long Olvera Street. It was a colorful Mexican marketplace complete with glassblowers, silversmiths, leather craftsmen, and candle makers. Everything spoke of the city's romantic heritage, and Catherine tried to imagine what it would have been like to have lived then, when there was so much to explore in the brave new world. She looked up at Nick and thought how much he would have loved the excitement of discovering new lands, opening up frontiers. If he had lived in that day and age, he very probably would have been a hero to be read about and studied through the ages.

She was so deep in her own reverie that she almost missed a very wondrous moment. They had walked through a historic adobe house and come out in its rear garden. Standing beneath the grape arbor, she was only half listening to Nick point out and name the native plants that perfumed the air with their sweet fragrances. It was then that it happened, at exactly 7:02. Nick reached down and took her hand.

Her heart stopped for a full second. It was a spontaneous thing, something he didn't even seem aware of, but Catherine was very aware of its significance. As they walked back across the wooden planks that led out of the house, she was sure he'd let go, but he didn't. Still holding her hand, he motioned toward the Pico House on Main Street.

Holding hands, Catherine thought, almost laughing, *we're actually holding hands.* It was such a simple thing. Something that she had taken for granted; until she met Nick. With the other men she had dated in the past, holding hands was nice. In fact, it was usually expected, but it just wasn't the sort of thing that Nick did.

Oh, Nick was very mannerly, a perfect escort. He opened doors, and he always walked on the outside. Catherine especially liked the way he touched her waist when it was appropriate that he guide or protect her. But hold her hand for no reason? Never. It just wasn't Nick's normal style.

Filled with an insurmountable joy, Catherine thought of how good, how right everything in the world had become. Nick made everything more colorful, more vital. She turned to him, a smile of sheer happiness on her face.

Nick squeezed her hand. "You won't believe this," he said as they left the Victorian-styled Sepulveda House and headed back toward Olvera Street, "but I actually thought ahead and made reservations at Casa La Golondrina."

Catherine was surprised, but she tried not to let it show. "Oh, that's great. I love their enchiladas."

He smiled and lifted his eyebrows, Groucho Marx style. "I've reserved us a quiet table for two by the fire."

"You know, Nick, tonight has me just a little worried."

"Why? I've been having a great time."

"Oh, I have, too. It's just, well, I don't know quite how to say this, but you're starting to act like a regular guy on a date."

He drew her hand up to his lips and kissed it. "When I'm with you, normal doesn't seem so bad. I like our quiet times." He shrugged. "I don't know, lately it seems I don't feel as compelled to run faster than a speeding bullet or to leap out of tall buildings in a single bound."

Relief sighed through her. "You've just made me a very happy woman."

"Now don't go getting your hopes up, I'm not—"

"I know, but it's nice to know that at least part of the time your feet will be on the ground. Now, come on, Clark Kent, I'm starving."

The fiesta atmosphere of the Plaza was carried into the restaurant, though mellowed slightly. Succulent smells spiced the air and mingled with the sound of strolling troubadours. They were shown to their table, and were just about to seat themselves when a familiar high-pitched voice called out, "Yoo-hoo!"

Nick stopped just as he was about to sit, straightened again, gave a low curse, then turned and waved to Bunny and Sidney. Catherine followed his lead, leaving out the curse, but by the time she had turned,

Bunny and Sidney were already barreling down on them.

"I was going to ask you to join us," Sidney said, pulling out a chair for Bunny. "But since you have a better table here by the fire, we'll just join you."

"Good idea," Nick said, giving them a tight smile. Then, facing the waiter who was standing by to seat Catherine, Nick added, "There will be four for dinner."

"Oh, isn't this just too cozy and romantic?" Bunny said, giving one of her famous giggles.

Catherine thought it was growing a lot less romantic by the moment, but she hid her disappointment behind the tall menu. After ordering, Sidney finally got around to the subject that Catherine knew was coming.

"Well," he said, "this is great luck running into you here."

"Yeah," Bunny said. "He's been trying to catch up with the two of you for a month now."

Sidney nodded toward Catherine. "I've stopped by Sunset at the Shore, and I've called, several times, but you were always out."

"Yes," Catherine said, offering no further explanation.

"You were always out with Nick of course."

"Of course," Nick repeated.

"You were either hang gliding or parasailing or some such nonsense. I believe once you were even climbing in the High Sierras."

Catherine glanced up. "Don't forget biking in Death Valley."

"I must have missed that one," he answered with disdain. Then his right eyebrow lifted in accusation. "Tell me, are you two dating, or trying out for the decathlon?"

Catherine laughed, Nick didn't, so she steered them back to Bunny's reference to the time. "I'll admit I've been in and out quite a bit, but it hasn't been a month."

Sidney bit into a crisp tortilla chip. "You're right, it's been a month and five days, but who's counting?"

"Oh, Sidney, you're exaggerating."

"Ooooh, no," Bunny said. "I've got everything written down here." She pulled a leather appointment book out of her purse. "Want to see?"

"No," Catherine said.

"I do," Nick said, taking the book from her and opening it to the current month.

"Don't bother," Catherine said. "I'm sure it's only been a couple of weeks."

Bunny reached across the table and tapped her frosted nail on the page to indicate the appropriate dates. "See, here was the awards ceremony, and then—"

"What's this entry?" Nick said, smiling slyly as he pointed to a day with little red hearts surrounding it.

Sidney rolled his eyes, but Bunny beamed with pride. "That was when Sidney and I started dating."

"Well, how about that," Nick said, handing the book back to her and winking.

"Yes, it started the night of the awards ceremony, and we've been a twosome practically ever since. And what about you two?" she asked, wrinkling her nose. "I saw those longing glances when you came in. I swear, Cupid must have been working overtime that night."

Nick nodded, then turned to Catherine. "They're right, it has been a month."

"Imagine that," Catherine said, having a sudden stab of guilt for ignoring her business so long. "My, my, time does fly when you're having fun."

Catherine sat back in her chair. But it had been fun. The most fun she'd ever had. Nick made every day so carefree, so exciting. She smiled suddenly, knowing what they meant by the phrase a month of Sundays.

"Well, you two. It's time to get your heads out of the clouds." Sidney reached down beside his chair and brought his briefcase up. Snapping the locks open, he pulled out a large handful of legal documents. "I expect to see both of you in my office, tomorrow. Catherine, we've got those certificates to discuss, and, Nick, I want to go over a clause in your—"

"Yeah, yeah," Nick interrupted. "I know. I'll be there."

"Well, see that you are. Don't you start—"

"I said, I'd be there," Nick snapped.

Bunny wriggled her fingers in front of Catherine. "I need to go powder my nose. Want to come?"

Still thinking about how frivolous she'd been toward her business, Catherine nodded mutely and followed Bunny. Once inside the ladies' room, she sat on a boudoir stool and stared into a large mirror that lined the wall.

"Catherine, can I ask you something?"

"Huh? Oh, yeah, sure." She snapped out of her guilt-laden thoughts and realized that Bunny was actually powdering her nose.

"It's girl talk, you know."

"Ask away."

"What would you do if you were in love with a guy, and he was really terrific, and you got along great, but he never talked to you? Oh, that was a silly way to put that, I mean, of course we talk, but Sidney never talks to me about the important things."

"Which are?"

"You know. His feelings, his innermost thoughts. I swear, he just keeps so much inside of himself. He never shares what he's thinking with me."

"Well, I doubt that he's ever going to pour his heart and soul out to you."

Bunny placed her hands on her hips and struck a dramatic pose. "And why not?"

"Some men just don't do that sort of thing."

"You said that Gideon did."

Catherine sighed with the warm memory. "Yes, he did, but Gideon was a rare man in a rare circumstance. You get pretty wise and wonderful when you know your days are numbered. Feelings become one of the most important things to you because while you're feeling them, you're still alive. Sidney hasn't been faced with that kind of harsh reality, so don't try to mold yourselves into being like Gideon and I were."

"Does Nick talk to you and share things?"

"Yes, and no. He doesn't open up a lot, but I've learned that if two people are attuned to each other, they'll hear each other even when nothing is said aloud."

Catherine stared into the mirror again, but she was seeing herself on top of a mountain, standing beside Nick and watching the sunrise. "With Nick, I've learned to watch for a look. It's a special look and it only happens at certain times, usually when we're both seeing something that he feels very deeply about. He'll look at me, and that one single look speaks volumes. In those moments I'm sure that I know everything that's important to and about Nick O'Donovan."

Bunny brought her finger to her mouth and tapped it against her pursed lips. "You know, I think I've seen that look on Sidney a couple of times. I mean, once when we were balancing his checkbook, I saw this look in his eyes and, well, it just told me so much about that big lug. I just threw my arms around him and—well, yes, I do know what you mean."

Catherine smiled. "Good."

When they returned to the table, the food was just arriving. As they began to eat, Bunny held court with a tale of a vacation she'd once taken to Mexico. Catherine wasn't listening. Her mind had returned to her intense involvement with Nick. An involvement that had made her act as irresponsible toward her business as she had once claimed Nick was to everyone and everything.

"A month," she muttered.

"Did you say something?" Nick asked hopefully.

"I was just thinking aloud. I just can't believe we've been running around like we were living in a dream world for the past month."

"I liked it. I think it's best when there are no tomorrows and no yesterdays, when only today matters."

"That moment to moment stuff is fine for a short time," Sidney said, "but it can't go on indefinitely."

"Right," Bunny said. "You see, when two people fall in love, they create this sort of fantasy world where only the two of them seem to exist. While it's easy to love each other in that world of your own making, you only know if it's true love when it's put to the test in the real world."

Everyone looked at Bunny in stunned silence.

"Don't you agree?" she asked.

"Oh, sure."

"Yes, of course."

She nodded. "You just can't believe I was the one who said it, can you?"

Sidney reached out and took her hand. "You never cease to amaze me, Bunny." Then, recovering from his moment of intimacy, he faced Nick. "Well, I guess you two will get your chance to test yourselves in the real world tomorrow."

Nick dropped his fork and shook his head.

"What's he talking about?" Catherine asked.

"You haven't told her? Oh, I'm sorry. I just assumed that you had."

"What?" Catherine asked again.

Nick signaled the waiter for the check then leveled a matter-of-fact look at Catherine. "I'm going back to work tomorrow for Spencer, as a stuntman in his new movie."

Chapter Eleven

Strains of marimba music followed after them as Nick and Catherine drove away from Olvera Street.

"I wish you'd say something," Nick said. "Go ahead, yell at me. Do anything except sit there looking so hurt."

"I just wish you had trusted me enough to tell me."

"I was going to, tonight."

"Is that why you took me on a normal date, to butter me up?"

"I took you there because it's one of my favorite places, and since you've made everything else we've done together so damn wonderful, I wanted to see if your magic worked there, too."

Catherine placed her elbow against the window ledge on the door and rested her head in her hand. "I'm sorry. I didn't mean to get tacky, but I'm hurt and angry."

"I don't blame you. I started to tell you earlier this evening, but you cut me off."

"Oh, Nick, what are we going to do about us?"

"The first thing is for you to stop being a D.D.H."

"A what?"

"A Damn Door Hugger. Scoot over here." She laughed and obeyed. He placed his arm on the back of the seat. "You feel so right in the crook of my arm, like you were made to fit there."

Smiling, she cuddled closer and lifted her head to look at him. "Was that a compliment?"

"Yeah. See, I realize now that I must have been walking around all my life like some giant jigsaw puzzle with some of my pieces missing. The funny thing is, I never knew they were missing, not until I met you. You filled in all the parts of me that were incomplete. Suddenly, all the pieces of my life fit together, and I wish there was some way we could mount and frame this moment, because I've got this real fear that I'm going to blow it."

"I won't let you blow it, Nick, and I won't let me blow it, either. If we work together, there's bound to be a way for us to both be happy."

"I don't want to lose you, Catherine. I don't want to be incomplete again."

"Oh, Nick," Catherine whispered.

They were both quiet for a moment, then Catherine noticed the wooded canyons. "Nick, this isn't the way to the beach. Where are we going?"

"I thought we'd go to my place for a nightcap."

"Is that all?"

"I certainly hope not," he said, smiling as they turned into his circular driveway.

It was a large Spanish-Mediterranean house, just off Mulholland Drive, and Catherine sat staring through the windshield at it. Nick came around and opened her door. She took his hand and let him help her out, but still her gaze remained on the house.

"You don't have to look so amazed," he said, leading her down a walkway that meandered through landscaped terraces of begonia and fuchsia.

Catherine looked at him. "I never imagined you had a place like this."

"A man's got to live somewhere."

"I pictured you in a bachelor's pad that doesn't require much commitment. Something, I don't know..."

"Something more temporary? Transient?"

She nodded.

He opened a set of ornately carved doors and they stepped into the marble-floored entryway. "Even a wanderer like me has to have roots somewhere. I finally gave in and bought this house. I love traveling, but sometimes when you're out there, it's nice to know you have a place to come home to." He slipped his arm around her waist. "Come on, I'll give you the grand tour."

The rooms seemed to flow from one to another by use of archways and alcoves throughout the house. Lots of teakwood and glass offered a sense of freedom and harmony that combined to make the rambling structure feel inviting. Along the tour, Nick had poured them each a glass of wine, and finally they ended in his bedroom, which had sliding glass doors that faced the valley.

Catherine stepped out on the deck that extended over the sloping hillside, and Nick followed her. They stood staring at the magnificent view, but Catherine's mind was back inside the house. He had finally brought her to his home, and she was overjoyed.

She hadn't noticed it at first, but lately one fact had begun to gnaw at her; in all the time they had been seeing each other, Nick had never taken her to his place. Catherine had rationalized to herself that his house was his last holdout. It was the one thing he kept to himself and didn't share. Though it hurt, she had accepted that for some reason he still needed a slight feeling of distance between them. His house had come to represent that distance, but now, he had brought her into his world completely.

With a sweeping motion of his arm, Nick indicated the hillside below them. "This mountainside is the studio back lot. It comes right up to my property line, just beneath this deck."

Catherine leaned her head on his shoulder as his arm slipped around her waist again. She gazed at the millions of twinkling lights that lit the valley beyond the studio grounds. "It's beautiful here. Truly."

"You know, I was thinking. I could walk to work tomorrow morning, it's just down the hillside. Then you could take the Woodie home and freshen up, then come by the studio for a while."

"Why?"

"I just thought it might help if you could see how it all really happens."

"I saw at the awards. It scared me to death."

"You weren't prepared. Besides, it's always frightening inside, in a small place, the illusion is more intense. But out on the lot, or on location, you can see the preparations, the calculations, and almost always the stunt goes as smooth as silk."

"Okay, Nicholas, I'll come, but I'm not promising anything."

"That's not my real name, you know?"

"What is?"

"David Selznick O'Donovan, but my dad hated the fact that my mom had named me after the director, so I was always just called, Nick."

She looked up at him and smiled. "You look more like a Nick than a David to me."

"I think so, too."

"Why did your mom name you after him? Did she know Selznick?"

"Sort of."

She cupped her palm as though to pull the story from him. "And?"

"She was a rather plain shy girl from the Midwest who came to Hollywood to find glamour. She found out, though, that it was going to take more than being a seamstress at one of the studios to make her life glamorous. I remember her telling me what a letdown it was when she finally got to meet some of the stars she'd idolized. They all turned out to be too human, too crude. But then Paul O'Donovan walked into her life.

"He had once been a star in some medium-budget pictures, but by the time my mother met him, he was middle-aged and a has been. He was known around the studio for trying to seduce every woman he met. Few responded, and of those who did, even fewer came back for more, but to her, he was flamboyant. She was just the boost his ego needed, too. She wasn't very pretty, but she was young, and she was starry-eyed, and she loved his exaggerated stories of his own self-worth."

"Then she got pregnant," Catherine said in sad anticipation.

"Yes, and Paul O'Donovan became scarce, at least until the gossip around the lot became so prevalent it was hurting what little name he had left. So he married her. That was when all illusion died. They moved into one of those awful stucco apartments that face a courtyard, which is required by law to have at least one dying palm tree. You've seen them, I'm sure."

Catherine nodded.

"Yeah, everyone's seen them. That's where the struggling young actors live until they can get a break, and where the struggling old actors die, wishing they had had a better break. God, I hated that place.

"Anyway, Paul continued to chase girls and drink. Did I mention he had a real alcohol problem? He did. They couldn't find him the night I was born, nor the next night, but guess who did stop by?"

"Selznick?"

"He was there to see a friend, but he ran into some of the people that used to work for him at Selznick International, and they mentioned mom was feeling kind of low, so he dropped by. He told her if she wanted to go back to work, meaning if she needed to support herself, he would assure her a place in the crew of his new movie. So," Nick concluded, "I was named after the nicest man my mother ever met."

"And did your dad ever show back up?"

"Off and on."

"I'm sorry, Nick."

"Don't be," he said, then lifted the drink out of her hand and set it on a deck table. "Now, would you like to tell me why we're standing out here talking about such nonsense, when we could be doing this?" He cupped her face with his hands and drew her to him. They tasted of each other in a slow deliberate kiss, but as always, their desire began to take over. Pulling back, they gazed into each other's eyes, then in a single movement, they turned and walked dreamily, into the bedroom.

Nick started to sing "As Time Goes By" while he unbuttoned her blouse. Catherine sang a line as she reached out and followed suit with the buttons on his shirt. Their clothes lay in a rumpled pile on the floor long before their duet ended. Even when they had stopped humming, they continued to sway back and forth in each other's arms.

Nick waltzed her to the bed, turned back the covers and together, they slipped inside the cool sheets. In the shadows the magnificent bone structure of Nick's face created an amazing play of light and dark planes. Unable to resist, Catherine began to smother his soft skin in an adoring succession of tiny kisses.

As she explored his face and neck with her tongue, her hands began to do the same over the hard muscled wall of his chest. Tired of her slow teasing movements, Nick took charge.

He rolled on top of her, never ceasing to wonder at the feel of her beneath him. He wanted to devour her, to possess her completely, and he caught her lips in a kiss that sought to make his wish come true.

He wanted to taste all of her, and together with his hands, Nick claimed every inch of her body. It was a body he had memorized. He knew every curve, every turn, and every response to his touch.

He shifted his weight until they fit perfectly together, and worshiped her face with kisses. Then, unable to resist the allure of her mouth another moment, Nick captured her lips again. She was his obsession, and he knew he would have no peace until he claimed her.

He gazed into her eyes, and saw their dark-green moons grow wide as she acknowledged the magnitude of the desire between them. He had to look at her, he had to remind himself that she was real and not a dream. He entered her and together, they began a slow sensuous climb toward the ecstasy that would soon consume them with its overpowering urgency. It was an exquisite search that was more fulfilling each time they explored the path.

Chapter Twelve

Catherine awoke with a start. Something was wrong. She was afraid to open her eyes and see what it was, but she had to. As if it would help, she only opened one eye. Early-morning sunlight was streaming through the open patio door and a shaft of light was spotlighting the empty pillow beside her.

She closed her eyes again. He was gone. It didn't matter that he had said he would be. There was still that instant before her mind clicked in, when only her heart was seeing—seeing the emptiness. She wondered if anyone who had never lost someone they loved, could understand how much it hurt. Slowly, sadly, she sat up and looked around.

Nick's room was so different from her bedroom. Gideon had given her a free hand in decorating, and she hadn't realized how feminine her touch was until she compared it to Nick's totally masculine decor. The room was full of leather and wood and warm earthy colors, along with an overall rugged-looking texture.

Oddly enough, she liked the feel of the room, if only Nick were there to complete the picture. Standing, she grabbed a robe he'd laid out for her. It was a dark-green velour with the elbows worn down to a shiny lime-green. As Catherine cinched it around her waist, his scent surrounded her. It smelled so completely of Nick that she turned to see if he'd come into the room. He hadn't.

Rubbing her arms, she stepped out on the deck and lifted her face toward the morning sun. It would be like this most of the time with Nick. His call at the studio would most always be before dawn. This was the real world they'd talked about, and it was lonelier than she had expected.

Feeling melancholy, she strolled toward the edge of the deck. The timing was incredible, for just as she reached the rail and looked down, she heard a muffled, "Action!" and suddenly World War II was taking place around her. Cannons were booming, bazookas blasting, and land mines were tearing the countryside apart as a hundred German soldiers came rushing up the hill, charging directly toward her.

Nothing else seemed to fit the moment better than for her to scream, but even as she did, the realization began to sink in. Then, as if to confirm her suspicions, a man peeked up at her from beneath the deck. He gave her a strange look, then placed his finger over his lips to indicate she should remain quiet, then he disappeared beneath the deck again. Shocked, Catherine stood on her toes and leaned as far over the rail as possible.

Her upside-down view was of an entire camera crew squeezed beneath the overhanging deck. Pulling herself up, she tightened her belt and headed back inside. "Hollywood!" she said, shaking her head. "We're definitely living at my place, if we ever make it that far."

As he said he would, Nick had a guest pass waiting at the studio gate when Catherine arrived. She parked the Woodie near Spencer's trailer, then started toward the area where Nick had told her they would be filming. She couldn't resist taking a small side trip through an area that was supposed to be New York, 1942.

Every time she visited the studio, Catherine fell in love with the magic of film. In spite of herself, she did understand why Nick enjoyed being a part of such a world. She sighed. If only he hadn't chosen the most dangerous job in the industry.

She stopped. *No, I will not think like that any more. I refuse. I love Nick. I want to be with him, and that's all that matters.* Starting down the street again, Catherine heard a siren in the distance, but she didn't pay it much attention. Sound effects were a way of life around a back lot.

Suddenly people began coming from every direction. Some were speeding in motorized carts, while others were on foot, bursting out of sound stage doors and running from sets. Everyone seemed to have the same destination, the same area where Catherine was headed.

She tried not to get caught up in the anxious atmosphere of those rushing past her, but soon found herself walking faster and faster. She'd overreacted so many times around Nick, and she was determined not to let it happen again. Everyone was probably just wanting to see the filming. Nick had told her they were going to try a new stunt. Then the ambulance, a real ambulance, streaked by her. Catherine tore out on a dead run.

"Oh, God, no," she kept repeating as she ran. "No!"

Finally, she got close enough to see a large crowd gathered inside an area that was roped off. Red flags waved in the wind, warning that it was a hot set, which meant that no one was allowed in, and that nothing was to be touched. Still, everyone was ducking under the ropes. Catherine did the same.

Shoving her way through the crowd, she asked, "What's going on? What's happened?"

"There was an accident while they were filming," someone answered.

"An explosion," said another.

Catherine didn't want to know, but she had to ask, "Was anyone hurt?"

"Yeah, maybe dead."

Catherine's legs went weak, but she pulled herself up as panic carried her through the throng of onlookers. Finally she reached the front of the crowd. A couple of official-looking men tried to keep everyone back, but Catherine broke through and started toward the area where the ambulance was parked. Dozens of people were clustered around the emergency vehicle, and she was sure she saw Spencer, bent over a stretcher.

She'd only made it a couple of yards away before a large burly man grabbed her arm. "You can't go up there, lady."

"I've got to!"

"You'll have to wait here, like everyone else."

"But Nick. My Nick, he's up there."

"Sorry."

"So am I," she said, delivering a swift kick to his shin.

The man let go of her and limped in a small circle, clutching his leg as Catherine shot across the rough terrain. She could hardly see through her tears, but she slowly began to realize someone was heading toward her. For a second she thought she was dreaming, but then she was sure. It was Nick, and he was running.

She needed so desperately to feel his arms around her, to be sure he was really alive, but her efforts seemed to only make her move more slowly. She couldn't get to him fast enough, but finally he embraced her wildly and swung her around until she was dizzy. Grateful tears mixed with their kisses.

"It's all right," he was saying. "I'm fine."

He put his arm around her shoulders and started away from the scene of the accident. Catherine was sure she couldn't have moved without him to lean on, and she couldn't stop crying. She was relieved and angry at the same time.

"Oh, Nick, I was so scared."

"I know. I'm sorry." He was smoothing her hair and wiping the tears from her face, continually trying to calm her.

She turned and faced him, grabbing his shirt. "It could have been you."

"It wasn't," he said, calmly.

"It might be next time."

"It won't."

"You can't be sure, Nick. You're not Superman. Something like this could happen to you."

"Catherine, honey, I know you're upset, but let me explain—"

She slapped his hand away from her face. "You can explain until you're blue in the face, but it won't change anything." She could feel herself on the verge of hysteria, but she had no reserves with which to fight it. "I can't stand it, Nick. I watched one man I love die, I won't watch it happen to you."

"Catherine," he pleaded. "Listen to me."

"No, you listen to me, Nick O'Donovan. I don't ever want to see you again. You can just go off and get yourself killed without me. I can't go through it again, I can't."

She turned and bolted down the streets of New York, circa 1942, but she became confused and ended up on a western set instead of near Spencer's trailer. By the time she found her way to the car, her tears were almost dry, and she had the hiccups. Opening the car door, she started to get in, then she saw Nick waiting on the passenger side.

"Get out of my car," she ordered.

"I know this is going to make you even madder, but this is my car."

He was right, it did make her madder. Catherine threw the keys at him, slammed the door and started walking down the street toward the main gate. Nick was walking beside her in an instant.

"Would you listen to me for just a minute?"

"No!"

He grabbed her shoulders and forced her to face him. "I want you to listen—"

"And I want you to listen. I never want to see you again!" she screamed, breaking free of him and dashing away.

She only heard the horn an instant before she looked up and saw the car coming at her.

Catherine's hospital room was filled with flowers, all beautiful, and all from someone other than Nick. She had a vague recollection of the ambulance ride from the studio, with Nick holding her hand. The nurses had said that he had paced in the waiting room while they set her leg, and then he had stayed by her side the rest of the day and all through the night. She couldn't remember, it was all a fog, a nightmare.

Nick had left just before they woke her for breakfast the next morning, and no one had seen him since. She'd had Spencer and Sidney and Bunny all looking for him, but two days later they all had the same report: no one had seen or heard from Nick.

She didn't know what to do, and felt utterly helpless being stuck in a hospital bed. What if he believed her foolish tirade? What if he never wanted to see her again? Fear gripped her. What if he was so upset that he sailed off around the world again?

"For a lady who was so anxious to get out of here, you don't look very happy," the nurse said, taking a final reading of Catherine's vital signs. "Aren't you going home this morning?"

Catherine nodded. "The doctor's already signed my release."

"Then why such a long face?"

"She's got man trouble," Bunny said, popping her blond head in the door.

Catherine waved Bunny in as the nurse gave a hearty laugh. "Honey, if the man you've got trouble with is the man I saw bring you in here, then, I say, fix that trouble fast!"

"I will, if I can ever find him."

The nurse had started for the door, but she paused. "He'll be back."

"Did he say that?" she asked, anxiously.

"No, but he will. I just know it. He's got it bad for you."

"I hope you're right," Catherine said as the nurse left, then to Bunny, "Any news?"

"Yeah, they lifted the smog alert."

Catherine shook her fist at Bunny. "After two days in here, I have no sense of humor. Is there any news about Nick?"

"Not yet, but Sidney's still out there looking. Now, come on, I've got to get you dressed and out of here. They're more strict about checkout time around here than a hotel."

Thirty minutes later Bunny was wheeling Catherine down the corridor when Spencer Lord came through the exit doors. "I'm glad I caught you," he said, "I just got a call from Nick—"

"Where is he? Is he okay? Does he want to see me?"

"I don't know. Yes. And yes. In fact, turn this little go-cart around because he said that he and Sidney would meet us on the front lawn."

"Why there?" Bunny asked.

"Who cares," Catherine said.

"I don't know," Spencer added. "He kept mumbling something about a balloon bouquet."

Catherine wished she could have leapt out of the chair and run to the front lawn, but her cast made it impossible. With a wry laugh, she patted the cast, as though apologizing for momentarily hating it. She didn't hate it, in fact, she was grateful to it.

Her broken leg had allowed her to understand what Nick had been saying all along; life is a gamble. She had finally come to believe that almost everything was dangerous, even crossing the street, but if love was on the other side, it was worth taking the risk.

Catherine was ecstatic as the automatic doors opened, but then she saw no one. "Do you see the Woodie?" she asked, searching the parking spaces around the circular lawn.

"No," Bunny said, "but don't worry, Sidney's always late for everything."

"He said he would be here," Spencer said, giving her a comforting pat on the shoulder. Then his hand froze. "Oh, my God."

"What?" Catherine asked, squirming around in the wheelchair. "Is it Nick?"

"Yes."

"Where?"

"Up there," Spencer pointed toward the sky above the lawn.

A hot-air balloon was descending toward the ground and Nick was waving from the basket. Tears of joy began to stream down Catherine's face, and she tried to stand. Spencer and Bunny steadied her as a landing crew of four men appeared from nowhere and began grabbing the ropes to lower the balloon gently.

"Get me out of here," Sidney cried.

"Get me in there," Catherine pleaded softly.

As Sidney jumped out of the gondola, Spencer and two of the men in the landing crew placed Catherine inside the basket which was filled with flowers. A relieved Sidney fell to his knees and began kissing the ground.

Nick smiled. "I hope you like my version of a balloon bouquet."

She threw her arms around his neck and kissed him. "I love your version of everything." Then she pulled back. "But can you fly this thing?"

"Are you kidding, I'm—"

She held up her hand. "I know, you're the best stuntman in Hollywood."

"Correction. *Was* the best. I've retired."

"No, Nick, I don't want you to change for me."

"I'm not. I'm changing for me."

Spencer touched Catherine's hand. "He's going to try a new career. I'm going legit. I'm tired of not having an Oscar, and I'm going to make movies that will at least get nominated."

"But," Nick added, "the money is in the action-adventure films. So Spencer is going to lend his name as producer, but he needs someone else to direct. I figured what the hell, why not give it a shot. I've been watching him do it ever since he started. I'm bound to have learned some things just through osmosis."

He put his arms around her and locked his hands at the small of her back. "I wasn't anywhere near that accident the other day. I'd already decided to pull out that morning. Spencer and I were discussing all this when the explosion happened."

Catherine wanted it to be true, but she had to be sure. "Nick, stunt work is your life. Maybe you should think about it. I don't want you to regret this later. After all, that kind of work is so much a part of you."

"It was a part of me, now you're a part of me. I don't need it any more. I finally have something to live for."

He signaled for the crew to release the ropes, and they started to rise. Catherine snuggled in his arms and smiled, then suddenly she bristled. "And just where have you been for the past two days, Nick O'Donovan? I was worried sick."

He pulled an official-looking document from his pocket. "I bought back the *Dangerous Lady* and I was busy getting her back in sailing shape." He placed the title in her hand and folded her fingers over the paper. "She's ready to go. All I need is a bride and we'll sail off into the sunset."

Catherine smiled. "The future Mrs. David Selznick O'Donovan prefers sunrises."

Silhouette Special Edition

COMING NEXT MONTH

#391 SOME WARM HUNGER—Bay Matthews

Once, Jessie Harper had put her career first and had turned down Bodie Lattimer's marriage offer. Years later, she was a first-rate horse trainer, a loving mother, yet an unfulfilled woman. Then Bodie came back to town....

#392 ALL THINGS CONSIDERED—Debbie Macomber

When her long-absent husband reappeared, Lanni Matthiessen was understandably wary. Judd soon proved mature, manly, worthy of her love. But with the fates—and his father—against them, could she keep Judd by her side?

#393 CHASE THE WIND—Rebecca Swan

Suffocated by urban life, Justine Fleming fled to rural Washington. Though high-powered Blair Sutherland needed her country comforts, his fast-track moves were taking her breath away!

#394 SNOWBOUND—Lisa Jackson

As teacher Bethany Mills reluctantly helped private eye Brett Hanson track down her criminal ex-husband, they forged a most uneasy alliance—until a blizzard trapped them in an avalanche of desire.

#395 TREASURES OF THE HEART—Anne Lacey

Lane Hartleigh wouldn't stand by and watch brawny demolitions expert Graham Randall destroy her beloved ancestral home. Against all odds she'd defend her treasure, but against Graham, could she defend her heart?

#396 CARVED IN STONE—Kathleen Eagle

Weary of being typecast, actor Sky Hunter retreated to the Rockies. Battling the elements, he had his chance to play hero to novelist Elaina Delacourte. But he soon learned that truth is far less predictable than fiction!

AVAILABLE NOW:

#385 FORBIDDEN FRUIT
Brooke Hastings

#386 MANDREGO
Tracy Sinclair

#387 THE MIDNIGHT HOUR
Jude O'Neill

#388 THE BABY TRAP
Carole Halston

#389 THE SUN ALWAYS RISES
Judith Daniels

#390 THE FAIRY TALE GIRL
Ann Major